GEA ASCENDING

BOOK 1: ETERNAL TWINS

To Tanya,

Mark John Terranova

December 13, 17

MARK JOHN TERRANOVA

outskirts press

Gemini Ascending
Book 1: Eternal Twins
All Rights Reserved.
Copyright © 2017 Mark John Terranova
v6.0

This is a work of fiction. The events and characters described herein are imaginary and are not intended to refer to specific places or living persons. The opinions expressed in this manuscript are solely the opinions of the author and do not represent the opinions or thoughts of the publisher. The author has represented and warranted full ownership and/or legal right to publish all the materials in this book.

This book may not be reproduced, transmitted, or stored in whole or in part by any means, including graphic, electronic, or mechanical without the express written consent of the publisher except in the case of brief quotations embodied in critical articles and reviews.

Outskirts Press, Inc.
http://www.outskirtspress.com

Paperback ISBN: 978-1-4787-7870-7
Hardback ISBN: 978-1-4787-7882-0

Cover Photo © 2017 www.thinkstockphotos.com. All rights reserved - used with permission.

Outskirts Press and the "OP" logo are trademarks belonging to Outskirts Press, Inc.

PRINTED IN THE UNITED STATES OF AMERICA

PREFACE

Gemini Ascending will introduce readers to a series of books written for those who wish *Game of Thrones* and *Lord of the Rings* never ended. This series will explore the mysteries of the Earth, the Universe and the subsequent power struggles, since the beginning, with exciting transitions between the past and present.

While each book in the series is a work of fiction, the storyline for each book will always be built around: scientific texts, articles and stories collected from key sources (see "Bibliography" and the "Special Section of Pictures" at the end of Book 1).

One source of stories, that will thread throughout the series, came from my father when he worked in Saudi Arabia, off and on, from February 1953 to December 1958. Throughout my childhood, teenage and adult years, I was always intrigued by new pieces of information that my father shared, as I grew older, surrounding the stories of: the punishments for crime, the broken Crane, Special Orders from the Minister, the railcar dinners with the Royal Family, the Parades, the King's interest in Locomotives, and the beautiful Date Gardens at Hofuf (more to follow in future books).

My science and engineering background along with personal experiences with different cultures and religions around the world has also led me to view the wonders of this World and the Universe in an introspective manner. Sharing such thoughts with the reader, throughout the storyline as it is developed, is a major reason for writing this series.

This series of books is for those who believe there is thoughtful purpose behind the creation of this World and this Universe.

Chapter 1

BORN

Early 1600's AD, North America

> *On the edge of darkness, the fading embers of carnelian skies linger in the horizon's crimson cry, and while drifting tufts of motif clouds wait to unveil another night's glistening starlight, Bay Moon eyes woo the oceans to sleep, and send its waves gently lapping upon the beach.*
> *MJT*

I have been told that the trauma of birth is buried deep within a being's psyche. Late one September evening, the fire of birth was upon me; my lungs burned for their first breath and the earth pushed hard against my chest, propelling me outward until I was released into cool ocean waters. Completely disoriented, like a new born turtle searching for safety, the moonlight became my beacon to the surface. I remember the starlit sweetness of the night greeting my face when I emerged. As air coursed into my lungs, I became aware of the power within my limbs and the knowledge encoded in my brain.

While I swam toward shore, the water cleansed my body and washed the last vestiges of birth from my long brown hair. Sitting on the beach, my skin blended smoothly into the yellow sand. Severely jaundiced, it would take several days of sunlight to heal me. Millennia had passed since beings of my kind were allowed to walk the face of the earth again; I was honored to be here, and, while I was naked and cold, the soothing night air and the gentle ocean waters that lapped upon the shore were mesmerizing. My affinity with the elements provided a joyous feeling.

Not alarmed by the footsteps that I heard crunching the sand behind me, for the cadence of steps conveyed no stealth or implied menace, I calmly rose to my six foot height, turning to see someone almost like me. He had long black hair, crisp alert brown eyes, an earthen smell, and light red skin surrounded by soft brown leather. Reaching his left hand towards me, with his rough fingers touching my face, I sensed his confusion; my body more than matched the musculature that he had, yet I appeared to be a young boy.

His smell changed an instant before I could react as his left hand grasped my long brown locks, pulling my head back hard while he raised his knife with his other hand. Although my hands quickly grabbed both his wrists, he knew my only weakness, squeezing even harder and pulling the very hair from my head. The pain was unbearable. Close to unconsciousness, abject terror was upon me; the unearthly screams that poured out from me only strengthened his resolve. Much weaker now, breathing slower, I let go of his wrists and looked into his eyes as I gave way to my fate. Tears streamed from my eyes—I was as helpless as any young boy would be under such an attack.

Staring at me until the tears stopped rolling down my cheeks, releasing my hair and sheathing his knife, he pulled me up from the sand and motioned for me to follow him. Further up in the sand dunes, he wrapped me in leather skins that he brought with him and made a fire. Listening to him talk, it was not long before I was able to speak his language, which made him slightly uncomfortable.

He told me that he thought I was an ocean spirit; such beings had come before. Most were evil and had brought death or long periods of pestilence to his village. He had visions of my birth for weeks during his meditations. His mother, a seer, along with the tribe's shaman had counseled him on the visions, how to determine if I was evil, and how to subdue and kill me if it was necessary — that is how he knew my hair was my weakness.

I asked him what signals I had given that caused him not to kill me. Laughing to himself, "actually," he said, "you gave me all the signs of evil: a boy with the strength of a man, screams of anguish that shook my spirit, and now the ability to quickly speak my language. These are all the signs. The only thing that saved you was your surrender to death and the pleading look that you gave near the end. Such things are more human; evil would have fought, snarling like a wounded beast to the very end. And that look in your eyes, I saw that same look in my young son's eyes years ago. He died shortly afterwards; perhaps that is what saved you the most."

Sensing the need for silence, I waited awhile before I spoke again, asking if he knew where I came from and what I really was. Admitting that he did not know, he suggested that the shaman and maybe even his mother might know. Although I knew the answers to these questions, I did not yet understand my purpose for being here; so, I had more questions to ask, but he suggested that we sleep. It was a long journey back to his village, and he would need his wits to convince the tribe that I was not an evil presence who had gained control of him. Before we slept, he handed me his knife and suggested that I cut all the hair from my head, which I did. If things did not go well at his village, he wanted me to be strong enough to escape his village alive, but he made me promise not to harm anyone if I had to leave.

It did not take long for me to earn the initial trust of the tribe.

Seeing a young boy of my size with my strength was alarming, but my poorly shaved head and jaundiced skin conveyed that I was ill, and perhaps somewhat human after all. It took a half moon cycle for my skin to heal and turn light red like theirs. I slept in the tent with my new father figure and his mother. His wife and baby had died in childbirth a few years ago; a little after that his only other child had also died, and he chose never to remarry or speak of these sad events in his life. The deep scars from cuts that he made in his arms conveyed the grief in his soul. Teaching me respect for all life and the love of nature, while also teaching me intelligent, efficient ways to fight and kill, I trained with the alacrity of youth while becoming a fierce warrior and an adept hunter. I liked this life, for it suited my sense of balance and being. It was the purest religion that I would ever know.

I never became sick or suffered the ills of any disease, healing very quickly whether or not my wounds were treated. More often than not though, I would seek out the healing powers and counsel of his mother, for she often talked to me as if I were part of her own family. In my second year with the tribe, we had a conversation that set the course of my life. Severely wounded from a hunt, I limped into her tent and fell on the skins that she had set out. She removed my clothes and slowly cleansed my entire body, rinsing my deep wounds with natural carboxylic acids and rubbing aloe from crushed leaves across all my skin abrasions. Strong tea made from various tree barks and natural flowers revived my spirit.

"You know," she started, "many young women have asked if they could learn how to heal like I do."

"Really? That is a compliment to your knowledge of healing; you should be proud."

She chuckled. "Well, it seems that the renewed interest in healing strongly coincides to your presence in this village. Many of the young women are quite enamored with your beauty, your alluring eyes, your strength, and the tales that the warriors tell of the hunt. They coyly inquire if you have expressed any interest in them. I tell them all to stay away from you — that you are as crazy as a rabid animal."

Somewhat offended, I yelped, "What? I'm not crazy! It's just that no man can match my fierceness in battle, or the speed and dexterity with which I overtake prey."

"Yes, but you are bored with your skills aren't you? I think that you seek more thrill in the hunt than is wise; is this why you attacked the boar yourself today?"

"It was the only fair way to hunt such a great animal — I couldn't mock his spirit. I used a knife in one hand, which actually hampered my movements, and it took many strokes to kill him. I could have broken his neck much faster with my bare hands, without all this injury."

"Have you really become that strong?"

Hesitating, with my eyes averting hers for a moment, I sighed. This was a moment of trust. These people had been so kind; I could not withhold the truth.

"Yes, I have become that strong, perhaps as strong as twenty warriors. I am afraid to let anyone know how powerful I really am."

"If that is true, then why do you act like you do?"

"Because my wounds still show that I am like them. I think this is all that keeps them from viewing me as a beast living among them."

"We know that you are different, but we also know that you have humanness in you. You are not an animal."

"I know that." I paused. "But will I become evil?"

Now it was her turn to be truthful. "The first time that I saw you, I was sure that you were evil. Your aura is solid energy, and you have no soul. I was convinced that you had tricked my son with your cunning. But as I observed you carefully over time, I realized that you were not a spirit, yet you possess the strength of one."

"So, do you know what I am, and what my purpose is for being here?"

"There is no word for you in our language, but our ancestors spoke of ancient ones like you: beings that are part human, who live many lifetimes, have tremendous strength, and are amorphous to their surroundings."

"I don't understand what you mean."

Softly, she murmured, "I mean that beings like you assume the teachings and lifestyles of those around you. Here in this tribe, you have learned love, respect for life, and how to fight and hunt only when the need arises. I am afraid that a being like you who was raised without such teachings would easily become evil—killing and ravaging without remorse. Without a soul, you have no voice inside you, no way of ever knowing what is right or wrong."

Speaking sadly, softly. "I have sensed that I live without a soul. When I look at the aura of other men and women, I see the difference between them and me: I can see their soul within the shell of their body. Some have such wonderful ones flowing within them—strongly rooted like trees, yet beautifully colored with flowers that grow wild in the fields. Others have dark, brooding souls, twisted like crabgrass."

"Yes, those souls will never attain peace until they learn to see beyond their own needs."

"But why don't I have a soul?"

Brushing his hair lightly, which was something she often did with her own son when he was young. "You were given life without one and that is your fate. It just means that when and if you ever die, your journey will end."

"How do you know that I will live a long time? You have hinted at this on several occasions."

"Your aura of energy says that you will live a long time. And look at your hands—they have no life lines—no beginning and no end."

"Then what is my purpose?"

"To be happy with life, as you have been during your time with us, and to find pleasure in living each and every day."

"I am happy, but I fear that I will never find peace."

A concerned look showed on her face. "Why do you say that?"

"Because if I stay in one place for a long time, people will suspect my immortality and begin to fear me; this will be my curse for life. That being the case, I do not think that I could ever have a wife or a family."

"Well, you will not have to fret over whether to have a family or not, for you will not be able to father children. You may enjoy the pleasure of love, but your seed cannot give life. I have seen this in you. However, imagine all the things that you will see, the things that you will be part of, and the course of things that you could change with your life. It will be amazing. You will not live in fear; you have nothing or no one to fear. Each day will be a new adventure! Can't you see how wonderful your life can be?"

"Yes, you have given me an insight into how special my life could be, and that makes me happy—thank you. But, I, uh, have one more question: which of the young women is really most interested in me?"

Smiling, she tossed the wet natural fiber cloth in my face and dumped all the cold water on my body. That day she healed me, giving me a sense of purpose for my entire life.

Many lifetimes later, I learned that I was born in the Delaware Bay and that the small peninsula next to my birth site would be called Lewes, (pronounced Lou's), Delaware. It would be a place of comfort and solitude that I would seek throughout my life. The last time that I visited Lewes, Delaware, I lived on the earth for hundreds of years, and my assumed name was now James Montgomery.

Chapter 2

THE DESERT

Islamic Year: 1377 AH   *1958 AD*

John Parella, Sr. was waiting for the Operations Minister to arrive. Passing the time, he found himself nervously leafing through his Arabic Work Vocabulary Book, which happened to be the 1946 second edition issued by the Arabian American Oil Company. Although a third edition had been promised for years, the training department that managed the editions had not quite gotten around to it yet. Flipping through the pages, he landed on his favorite pair of translations that were right on top of each other on page 33 of the text:

"the empty money bag" translated to "kiis al fuluus al khaali".[1]
"the big oil company" translated to "sharikat az zait kabiirah".[2]

Someone in the training department had quite a sense of humor as the big oil companies would always strive to empty everyone's money bag. Perhaps this little faux-pas is why a third edition was never approved.

Hearing a commotion outside the office, he knew the

Minister had arrived. His Excellency had been the Deputy of Oil Operations for years. His office had never questioned previous orders or purchases in the past, yet this latest transaction had obviously concerned the Minister enough to warrant an official visit from Riyadh.

John thought about his activities over the last month. As grade Master Mechanic, he was chosen to go to Essen, Germany to inspect a 155 freight car order and all the ancillary equipment at the Ferrostaal Company. Upon his arrival in Düsseldorf Airport, he was met by the Managing Director and Chief Engineer of Ferrostaal; they reviewed the schedule for the week, and promptly started the inspections the next morning. Since the Ferrostaal Corporation had many subsidiaries across Germany, it was necessary to travel to several cities to finish the inspections. The petroleum and asphalt tank cars were inspected at the Prometheus Works in Hanover. Wheel sets were inspected at the Georsmarien Works in Osnabruck, along with the truck side frames that had been built in Belgium and sent over. He had even visited the Glassing and Scholler Company in Dortmund to review research and development there on a special set of fiber brake discs to combat brake erosion caused by the sand. The only hitch to the whole trip was that Westinghouse had not completed the manufacturing of all the triple valves specified in the order for the petroleum and asphalt tank cars. Because the schedule for getting the freight cars on line was very tight, he approved the entire order along with the installation of standard valves and agreed to field install the triple valves for a reasonable price reduction. All parties were pleased with the results of the trip, and he returned to Dammam.[3]

The Minister, in addition to three body guards, walked into the field headquarters and whisked past him without acknowledging his presence. The bodyguards were dressed in the traditional white garb with a black headband holding their white turbans in place. Each guard had two daggers sheathed in leatherpockets at opposite sides of their waist, with leather gun straps and holsters diagonally cutting across their chests making an X with the leather straps that held their spare bullets.

The minister also had a white turban with a black band, but he wore a white cotton shirt with a gray cotton suit under a white cape. This ensemble, coupled with his mustache, goatee and sunglasses, created a formidable presence. Fifteen minutes later, John was called into the office to speak to the Minister.

Walking into the office, he was at least grateful that two fans were turning in this room, because the outer office was stifling. Although he had been in Saudi Arabia for nearly five years, he had never acclimated to the heat as the Saudis had. The minister, who was sitting in a chair behind a rather plain, sturdy metal desk, motioned for him to sit down, at which point he noticed that the stiffest chair in the room had been brought over for him to sit in. This did not bode well for the conversation about to take place.

"John Parella Senior, is that the correct pronunciation of your name?"

"*Na'am,*" meaning yes, he replied, confirming the way to pronounce his name.[4]

"Well, John Parella Senior, may I assume that we can hold this conversation in Arabic?"

"Actually, no. I mean, *la.*"[5]

"What a shame; here I have mastered your English language, and you have been over here several years, and yet you do not speak Arabic."

John chose not to answer, and after a few awkward seconds passed, the minister proceeded.

"I am told that you have reached the rank of Master Mechanic, which is quite an accomplishment for someone so young. You are twenty-seven years of age, are you not?" This was clearly a rhetorical question.

"In addition, I am told that you treat Arabs with a great deal of respect: that you honor most of our customs and that you even provide letters of recommendation for hard-working trainees who do not pass the school work or the field work. This is somewhat irregular for a westerner. Why are you so different?" This time the minister was expecting an answer.

"Respect is the most revered compliment one individual can pass onto another. Whether a person is young, old, rich, poor, or slightly different in any way, respect is the one universal constant that all individuals seek."

The minister was taken aback. "Am I in the presence of a great philosopher? I am told that you have little formal education. How did you acquire such a philosophy on life?"

"My knowledge comes from life experiences; such things are not necessarily taught in schools."

"Well, I certainly agree with you on that point John Parella Senior, but where in your life did you acquire such knowledge?"

John's forehead was perspiring, for he had not anticipated such a line of questioning. The minister had sensed how uncomfortable he was becoming. John took a deep breath before attempting an answer, and the minister smiled.

"Our family was very poor when they came to America from Italy. Hard work, honesty, giving and earning respect accordingly, and applying a strong fist when necessary provided the path to the knowledge that I have."

At this the minister removed his sunglasses. Leaning forward he spoke with a hint of curiosity, "If I closed my eyes and listened to such words in Arabic, I would swear that you were Islamic. So you are a believer? Do you pray each day? Do you go to your Church on *yaum al aHad, Sunday*?"[6]

"I speak to my God by my actions each day."

"A westerner who actually practices their religion instead of attending ostentatious weekly rituals, I am impressed. Now tell me more about this fist of yours. I was told that you were a boxing champion on your ship in the Navy; judging by the size of your arms and physique, I could believe this, but you are a bit short to box—five feet nine inches, yes?"

"I was the champion on my ship when I was seventeen,

besting many other ship champions, many of whom were men almost twice my size. Strength is important, however, agility and strategy combined with strength are the ultimate tools inside the boxing ring. There were some who were better than me though, and they won my respect."

"Well, I must admit that you are not what I expected. That is good. Now that I know you better, I would like to move onto the purpose of my visit. I read the trip report that your supervisor, Mr. Jiling, sent to my office. You did an excellent job in your inspections in Germany; I was quite impressed with your work. However, I became concerned over Item 7 of the order. Item 7 called for ten miles of track complete with custom turn-outs, 51,500 ties, drilled to fit a unique tie plate that handles almost twice the load normally specified, and over 50,000 special type T rail anchors."[7]

"In fact, I became so intrigued that I found it necessary to ride out here to speak to you personally on this matter. As Minister, I also expect to receive respect from the employees that we hire. So, would you please explain why I should spend all this extra money on ten miles of non-standard ties and track? Where do you intend to lay this track, and what is it that you intend to haul over this track?"

Well, this was it: the exact scrutiny that he had hoped would not be discussed when he heard that the Minister wanted a personal visit with him. Reluctantly pulling a somewhat sweat-soaked envelope from his shirt pocket, he handed it to the minister. It was an official sealed envelope of the Saudi Government Railroad Operations with red and blue parallelograms bordering the perimeter of the envelope on each side. The minister was not pleased with this development, and was clearly caught off-guard. Glaring at John, anger was threaded in the next words that he spoke.

"So, is it true, you had an audience with the King?"

John did not respond.

After opening the envelope and reading the letter inside,

the minister handed both items back to John. Staring at him for close to thirty seconds, the minister then asked him if he had witnessed the punishments carried out yesterday. Clenching his jaw, John glared back at the minister. Two guards moved forward towards John, but the minister quickly waved his hand.

"Mr. Parella, as I will now call you, my guards are trained to read body language and react immediately; they do not err on the side of caution. I suggest that you refrain from further disdain for my questions."

John was irate, but he knew his situation was precarious. It was the aid of the Minister himself who had told John that he was to witness the punishments yesterday.

"Yes, I saw them; several hands and feet were strung up on a rope that morning. In the afternoon, a murderer was beheaded right on the street."[8]

"Good, good, now perhaps you have a better understanding of Arab law and justice. We are really a peaceful people, but when a wrong is committed, the wrong is corrected. Steal and you lose a hand; continue to steal and you lose your feet; if you murder, then you lose your head. Our crime rate is quite low. Is this not the same in America?"

The minister wanted no answer; so, he continued.

"You have to realize that our history is one of defending our way of life and that which is ours with our very lives. The values of our way of life apply to every person, whether they are a common person, a King, an Imam, or a government official. Therefore, when a Sheikh believes that someone is seriously disregarding their obligations, or disrespecting them, as you would put it, then he is obliged to correct the situation. Do I make myself clear, Mr. Parella?"

Without waiting for an answer, the Minister rose from his chair and continued speaking. "You are to destroy that envelope and the letter today. Perhaps you can burn them in the still that you keep in your back workshop, which you will also dismantle today. Such things are forbidden in Saudi Arabia, and you had better learn the formal greeting and response expected in Arabic. Whenever you are in my presence again, or the King's presence, such respect is required." After that, the minister and his bodyguards left.

Chapter 3

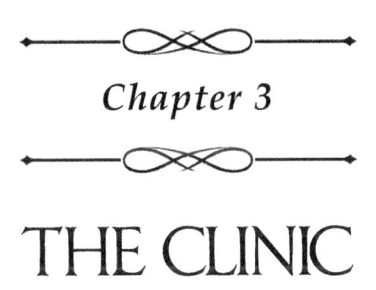

THE CLINIC

Chadds, Ford, Pa.　　　　　　　　　　　　　　　*May 1995*

The day began with such beauty. The morning dew brought a sparkle to the grounds. The redolent embrace of fresh cut grass lingered in the crisp, cool air. Cardinals and blue jays fluttered among the birch trees and small saplings bordering the estate, while a light fog still clung to the valleys and hillocks below. John Parella, Jr. continued to watch the day unfold from his second story window. Gardeners were tilling the flower beds, preparing the soil for the annuals that were unloaded the day before. They were systematically working the Western and Northern flower beds at the moment. In the afternoon, they would attempt to work in whatever shade they could while finishing the flower beds across the entire estate.

He shifted his gaze to the walls surrounding the estate. While all the main buildings on the estate were constructed with solid, strong, blue stone from the Malvern quarries, the walls surrounding the estate were an elegant blend of field stone. Twenty-two years ago, as a boy of sixteen, he remembered hand mixing the mortar for the two masons who built the outer walls.

Unable to recall their names, he remembered the older mason telling him on more than one occasion how to mix the mortar properly.

"Twelve batches a day, kid: two bags of cement, and thirty-two shovels of sand per batch. Mix it well and don't water it down. The mortar has to cling tightly to the trowel when I scoop it and shake it."

Although all masons that he worked with were finicky, the old man and his son were true artisans. Each morning, he would watch them walk through all the field stone, spread out on the ground, and select the rocks for that day based on color, texture, and size. When laying a course, if a stone did not add the right balance to the wall, the old man would toss the offending rock away. He would then stand there and mutter to himself until his son brought back a few selections that might work. When it came time to point the stone, the older mason would only let his son mix the mortar, and then they would both press and shape the mortar to the pointing that they had selected. John watched them point the stone for three days, washing off their tools and handing them whatever they needed. The older mason smiled and said that John's work would soon come. On the fourth day, he brought a bag of wire brushes, endless gallons of muriatic acid, and a garden hose. John spent the rest of the summer meticulously scrubbing off the excess mortar that dripped onto each and every stone, and he loved every minute of it, or so he told everyone else. The end result was exquisite outer walls, rivaling stonework that he had seen in early American cities; John had no doubt that it would stand the test of time. He was, on the other hand, very skeptical whether his life's work would produce the same overall result.

Moving away from the window, John glanced at the clock on the nightstand. If he was going to get a jump on the day, he would have to get going. Turning the porcelain handle on the gold faucet, he looked in the mirror. The face staring back at him was a far cry from a youth of sixteen. There was still some luster in his thick, wavy dark black hair, but he was overweight, which showed in the puffy checks on his face. His brown eyes retained their sexy softness, and he still had a hearty laugh that made everyone around him happy when they heard it, but the dark circles around his eyes conveyed a weariness that was, at times, disheartening and well beyond his years.

Using the hot water, he took his shaving brush and lathered the soap for his face. Grinning when he picked up the shaving brush because it just had a few bristles left, it looked more like a mortally wounded toothbrush. His father had given it to him when he was thirteen he could never throw it away, as some things have untold sentimental value. Sentiments on shaving ended there though; with the facial stubble that greeted him each morning, he was happy to own a double bladed razor.

After shaving, John Jr. slapped on the clothes that he laid out the night before, along with his Converse sneakers. No one would ever accuse John of being fashion conscience; his clothes were often wrinkled, and color coordination was definitely not his forte.

Clearly in a funk and having been this way the last several months, he also knew that more psychiatric therapy and pills were not going to fix this situation. A deep depression was already setting in this morning the more he reflected on his life at the clinic and his life in general. He had been counseled to recognize the triggers that caused depression and to try to work through them, but it was not working as it once did.

He tried to cheer himself up as he left his room. After all, it was his birthday later this month, but while walking down the hallway to the cafeteria, no one would wave or say hello; his tirade the night before at supper still had everyone upset, and that morose feeling of self-pity was setting in hard. Knowing that a change was needed was one thing, yet finding the courage to make a change was quite another matter.

Strolling through the buffet line, he added items that he had eaten the last several days for breakfast. Even eating a good meal no longer made him happy. Gobbling the food down in ten minutes, without really tasting anything, he made his way to the exit door.

The Clinic was part of the southern complex, which comprised psychiatric care units and behavioral science units. The northern complex was used for biomedical research. The facilities at the western end of the complex were dedicated to the sciences, compromised of microbiology, organic and inorganic chemistry. The eastern complex was dedicated to long term grants and privately funded research. The complex also had one very large administrative building right in the center of the entire estate.

John took a moment for some dark humor. During his high school summers, he helped build many parts of this complex. After college, he had worked in the biomedical complex and in the labs at the western end. After working there for five years, he branched out on his own. Using a large amount of his own money from his inheritance and some venture capital money, he started a company focused on developing unique biomedical applications from organometallic compounds. He and a few close colleagues worked out the chemical sequencing, writing the patents for these materials over a seven year period. John's failing marriage caused him to think about selling his control of the company to the venture capital group, against all advice from his wife, private paid consultants, and his colleagues. He grossly underestimated the net present value of the patents that he and his colleagues worked on. John Jr. just seemed to have that knack; ninety-nine out of one-hundred people would see a set of facts one way, and John would see it the other way. Some labeled it as eccentric brilliance; others called it the curse of no common sense. After selling the business, his colleagues were ousted shortly afterwards. The venture capital group then made hundreds of millions on the company resale a few years later. His colleagues and their spouses found it impossible to speak to him and his wife. With his wife's close friends now alienated from her, this was indeed the last straw in a disintegrating marriage. Now, he was back at the complex in the psychiatric care unit, having come full circle; life was indeed ironic.

The entire site, and the organization that ran the complex, was founded in 1964 by Mr. Theodore Preston, a native Pennsylvanian, whose vision was to pull some of the best minds on the East Coast to this site for research and development that had practical implementation windows. "And," as Mr. Preston would joke, "perhaps a few minds from the West Coast, if we really get desperate." Wanting Chadds Ford to be more than a national treasure as a historical site, he also wanted it to be renowned nationally for the highest levels of intellectual implementation. To turn his dream into reality, results would matter; this campus would have to do more than publish papers. It was not just a think tank, and ideas would have to be tested, validated, implemented and sold. To this end, Mr. Preston established the foundation with a board of trustees and 80 million dollars in seed money, which was used to build, facilitate and maintain all the buildings and property to the specifications required of the tenants; no rent was ever charged for facility use. However, if a project did not deliver on its commitment window, then the entire project team was literally out in the cold. The waiting list to get in was more than long; it made every university and industrial complex area in the country green with envy. Revenue for the site was created from the psychiatric unit as well as from lucrative licensing and revenue sharing agreements between the board of trustees and tenants when their ideas were patented, implemented, and sold. The administrative building housed the lawyers, accountants, and clerks that tracked the forecasted revenue versus the actual accrued revenue received down to the penny.

Making his way across the lush lawns to the walls bordering the complex, he started walking along the perimeter of the estate, while still marveling at the architectural foresight of the complex. From his vantage point, the patina on the copper roofs and gutters blended in perfectly with the ivy that had crept up on the Malvern blue stone buildings. Mr. Preston had insisted that all buildings be constructed this way, and that no building, except the administrative building, was to be more than three stories tall, which made the entire estate look architecturally like an eighteenth century village, with a town hall proudly displayed in the center. However, on many occasions, Mr. Preston would facetiously state that the lawyers and certified public accountants in the administrative town hall building really did need five stories—two stories to count all the money and three extra stories for all those egos.

As he approached the eastern end of the complex and his ultimate destination, tears formed in his eyes. Beyond these estate walls were acres of soft needled evergreens flowing along the hillocks that sloped downward to the Brandywine River. This river slowly ambled its way past large farms and old single lane wooden bridges until it continued its journey down into Delaware. Having swam, canoed, walked, and run with his Irish Setter on the banks of this river on many occasions, the solitude and peacefulness of those jaunts always cleared his mind. John ached to roll back the years and run along the Brandywine with his dog in simpler times. Life was either getting too complex, or he was just having too hard a time adjusting to the life that he had, or perhaps he really had no real desire to work at anything anymore.

Looking over toward the main entrance, he saw the guard open the steel gates, and recognized Dr. Ashe's green Porsche right away, which he followed as it traveled past the administrative building and veered left to the clinic. Dr. Ashe felt daring today, parking at the front of the building right in Dr. Junger's parking space; something he would not dare do if Dr. Junger were not away at an international conference. As Dr. Ashe exited his car with a large coffee in one hand and a bag of Dunkin' Donuts in the other hand, he walked the distance to the front doors of the clinic with a happy, light gait.

John was sure that he would shortly ruin Dr. Ashe's day, perhaps his whole week.

John came to the highest section of wall on the eastern edge of the complex. For weeks in his daily walks, he had noted the footholds and handholds that would allow him to scale this section of wall. In two minutes, he was standing on top of it. The estate guards arrived shortly thereafter; their Two-Way Motorola radios were blaring back and forth to the main office. He heard Dr. Ashe screaming into the radio. His voice kept getting clipped, because he was speaking before pressing the push-to-talk button on the radio.

"…at do you mean, he is talking to someone up on the wall? Who else is there?"

The guard answered, "Well, I can't see anyone there, maybe they're on the other side of the wall."

"…ust get him down, now!"

"I can't Dr. Ashe; he doesn't even acknowledge that we're here."

"..ust wait there until I get there, and keep him on the wall."

At last, John saw the portly Dr. Ashe walking briskly, and then attempting to run across the grounds; he was completely out of breath even before he got half way. It looked like he had spilled coffee across his lab coat and mashed half a doughnut on his shoe. It was quite comical, and John might have even laughed if he had not been so focused on the task at hand. As Dr. Ashe neared the wall, John spread both arms out and let himself fall forward. Flowing through the first evergreen trees, the large branches bent gently at first, but then they started to snap in rapid succession as his velocity increased. Preparing for the fall, his body tensed, just as his back slammed hard into the ground, sending intense painful shock waves, until he twisted his ankle so hard that he screamed. Continuing to roll down the hill, muscles all over his body became deeply bruised. When he thought that he couldn't take any more, he somehow remembered TV commercials stating to young kids and teenagers: "to never try something like this at home," after which his head slammed into a rock, rendering him unconscious.

Chapter 4

MARRIED

At 5:42 AM, James Montgomery awoke startled; a little groggy, he couldn't quite figure out what woke him up. Sitting upright, seeing their Sheltie sleeping soundly in the foyer next to the boy's room, the house seemed quiet, and there were no loud noises outside, yet something was out of place. Perhaps it was just the hubbub of the last twenty-four hours catching up with him. He and SuiLeng, his Chinese wife, had gotten married yesterday, after being together for nearly three years, and knowing each other for almost twelve years. Getting out of bed, wrapping his robe around him, he went to check on the boys. Watching them sleep, each of them nestled in their own blankets and pillows, breathing slowly without a care in the world, was always a joy, and that was the way it should be. Though they were not his own children, he had grown to love them with an affection that might have rivaled their natural father's love while he was alive.

Returning to his bedroom, he eased back into bed hoping to get back to sleep. Watching the fan slowly turning near the ceiling, smiling as he remembered their wedding night, they had promised the minister to remain celibate three weeks beforehand, which made last night a special, yet anxious, celebration of their love. After getting the boys to bed, they exchanged presents, making private vows to one another, which was a tradition in SuiLeng's family that James became enamored with when he heard how many generations had honored this tradition. After sharing their vows, they unrobed in front of one another and joined together in tender kisses with long embraces. When their passion welled up, James picked up SuiLeng and carried her to bed. Taking each of her hands and putting them behind her head, he romantically brushed her lips with his until their breath could not hold any more anticipation. Then he intimately kissed and slowly caressed her body until she moaned as her entire abdomen rippled with pulses of pleasure. Lying next to her, words of love were spoken, but she would have none of it.

Pushing him away while looking deep into his eyes, she replied, "Just remember, my love, you started this, and you should never start a fire with an Asian woman that you can't extinguish." A flame had been lit within her.

She was on top of him the next second, straddling his hips, sharing a mixture of passion, love, and lust while controlling every motion and emotion for the next several hours until he begged her to stop.

"Stop?" she exclaimed. "Are you kidding me, you wuss. Ah, you men are all the same; women can make love so much longer. We were just getting started!"

James was up off the bed limping around. Both his buttocks and glands were throbbing; he would spend the next forty-five minutes trying to walk it off. Watching him the whole time, laughing and playing with the covers, she exposed certain parts of her body, teasing him. Finally admitting defeat, he asked if they could go to sleep now. She said that she would consider it; however, if he misstepped one little bit in the future after that, she would show no mercy.

SuiLeng was all woman, the only type of woman that he could

be with; she was tough, confident, decisive most of the time, and quite a lover. James remembered the first time that she really saw him as he was, which was at a restaurant in Penang, Malaysia. He was eating pepper crab and drinking beer all by himself at a large table near the water when he saw her move towards him. Swaying back and forth after drinking one too many Mai-Tais, she was looking deeply into his eyes the whole time. Encountering such situations before, he had learned to subconsciously scan the crowd and listen for any soft footsteps near him. When his keen sense of hearing detected nothing but the sweet susurration of the warm Malaysian breezes, he knew that he was completely safe in her company. She continued walking, and then sat down right next to him.

Still staring into his eyes, she said, "I know what you are; I see your entire aura. It's all crimson, tinged with teal. My grandmother told me of such auras, but I never imagined that I would meet such a being."

James was more intrigued than unnerved; it had been many years since anyone was astute enough to really see him as he truly was. Most amazing was that she was not repulsed by what she saw.

Without asking, she took his hands into hers; he was mesmerized by her boldness. Looking at his palms, "You have no life lines on your hands at all. What does this mean; is this natural for you, or did you have this done on purpose?"

Her curiosity was insatiable; she asked more questions than he could dare answer, but his acute senses told him that she was sincere. Holding her hands, he became aware of her aura along with the sixth sense that the women in her family possessed and passed down from one generation to the next. He answered some of her questions.

"My aura is not unique, but there are only a few like me that exist, and it is natural for beings like me to have no life lines. It just means that we can live a very long time."

She just sat there, blithely staring at him for several more minutes. Then, somehow, and he could not remember how, SuiLeng steered the conversation toward much lighter subjects.

She ordered food for herself in Cantonese. Her parents had moved from Hong Kong to Malaysia years ago, and while mainland China spoke Mandarin, the prevalent language in Hong Kong was Cantonese. When the shark fin soup came, she told James about how the shark fins were harvested, how the soup was made, and the virility that her ancestors believed was derived from it.

James was appalled at how the shark fins were simply cut off the shark, and the shark was then thrown back into the water. Telling SuiLeng about the American Indians, he stated how they honored the spirits of the animals that they killed; how they used every bit of the animal, and said prayers in its honor for the gift given.

When James finished his quaint diatribe, SuiLeng countered that the Chinese culture is thousands of years old, that the Chinese believe that anything with its back to the sun is allowed to be eaten, and she was sure that this also applied to smart-ass *Gwai Los* like himself.

Her brazen manner made him burst out laughing. When the local fruit came, consisting of water melon, papaya, and mangos, she politely stated that the papaya and mangos were for her. Watermelon was for Westerners, "You know, those people with little acquired taste."

James ate most of the fruit; so, SuiLeng ordered some durian for both of them. After this experience, he had to admit that he could do without durian his entire life—it had the texture of sandpaper and smelled like an elephant's backside.

They spent the weekend together at the Rasa Sayang Hotel. In the morning of their first day together, they walked along the beach, absorbing the beauty of local life. The fishermen had their boats pulled up on the beaches, and their nets were hung to dry while they playfully jawed at one another during their chess matches. Walking past the hotel and the hawkers market set up along the beach, they admired the teak wood construction of the local homes. SuiLeng commissioned a batik cloth from a local girl. The girl who made it told SuiLeng the symbolism within the picture: the beach, palm trees, and the moon depict the simple yet balanced life that the natives have with nature. That evening they ate at the Feringgi Grill in the hotel. This time James ordered the food, requesting Australian cuts of beef in grams along with a Caesar salad, where the dressing was made from scratch at the table. A split of champagne started their first course, and several bottles of Chambertin Montrachet brought perfect harmony to the meal. SuiLeng was impressed, questioning him on how he had acquired his taste for food and wine.

Remembering how his cocky grin conveyed all the answer that was necessary, they were wild in bed, and their passion and excitement flowed for hours—the passion of discovery and the excitement of being discovered. Ecstatic after he found out that she lived in the States and that she was just visiting her family in Malaysia, they agreed to see one another when she returned from her trip.

Dating on and off for years and becoming very good friends, SuiLeng only found one other man with the confidence of James; she married him, but he passed away from an illness. James, on the other hand, also had tragic memories of a lost love.

At 6 AM, James eased over to his wife and gently stroked her hip while kissing her ear. Grabbing his hand and softly bringing it to her breast, she turned, kissing him passionately. They looked into each other's eyes and made love gently one more time before the boys woke up.

The next several hours for John Parella, Jr. were a hazy dream. Voices streamed in and out; some voices were excited, yelling, other voices were soothing, asking questions that he could not quite understand or answer. He even thought that he heard Dr. Ashe crying for a period of time. He felt a soft cloth under his head. For a moment, several sirens filled the air around him, then gentle fingers turned his legs and arms slightly. Many concerned eyes looked down at him before he was lofted into the air and placed inside the ambulance. More voices came and went. Voices were all around him, voices inside his head, voices he knew. At one point, John even thought that he heard his mother's voice, but he was only remembering an earlier accident that happened when he was six. More voices and incoherent moments were followed by many longer lapses of unconsciousness. The voices faded, followed by silence.

James decided to go downstairs and get the coffee pot going. SuiLeng loved coffee; he was a tea drinker, but even James appreciated the aroma of fresh brewed coffee in the morning. With the coffee brewing, James strolled outside to get the morning paper. Walking down the drive, he always marveled at the year round South Florida scenery: pastel homes, blue skies, green grass, date palms, a plethora of queen palms, and a few royal palms created the ambiance of his neighborhood. Others enjoyed the temperate climate in Florida from November through March each year, but his physiology ached to absorb the blistering heat in the other seven months of the year. Basking in the sunlight, converting its energy to rejuvenate his body, was one way his kind maintained their immortality.

Carrying the newspaper back into the house, James went to the intercom and tuned the built in radio to the news channel. A few seconds later, he heard a headline that made him tremble:

"SUICIDE ATTEMPT AT THE CLINIC IN CHADDS FORD, PENNSYLVANIA INVOLVING ONE OF DOCTOR JUNGER'S PATIENTS. John Parella, Jr. was the second person to attempt suicide *at the noted Clinic in the last three years. Apparently Mr. Parella had jumped before..."*

Ignoring the rest of the news clip, his six foot, 123 kilogram Herculean body shook for the first time in fifty years. Sitting down at the kitchen table, he ran his hands across his clean shaven head. His hazel eyes burned, and his breathes were short. He was snorting through each nostril as a bull does within the ring, waiting for the matador to make a move, mind and body yearning for action, yearning for the fight.

Walking over to the desk in the front room of his home, he pulled open the top drawer and removed his favorite stones. Sitting in the desk chair, he closed his eyes and rubbed the soothing Ocean Jasper in his left hand and the Howlite in his right hand, immediately feeling the energy within each stone, energy from the beginning of the universe that was harnessed over billions of years within these stones. SuiLeng and the boys represented a complication that must be considered and reconciled within present events.

The phone rang, and SuiLeng yelled down for him to pick up. He knew exactly who was calling, and who was about to call.

Chapter 5

THE HOSPITAL

John Parella, Jr. awoke in a private room with the morning sun draped around the iron bars in the window next to his bed. The night nurse was checking the IV needle in the front of his left hand; he watched her add a new bag of D5W to the IV pole, after which she attached an empty bag to the catheter tube. As she walked back from the medication cart, she told him that this would be his last injection of painkiller now that he was awake.

"What kind of painkiller is that?"

"Demerol."

In a sarcastic yet serious tone, he said, "What, no morphine?"

"You can take that up with the doctor; he will be on rounds shortly."

Seeing straps across his body, a soft cast around his right ankle, a wrap around his left arm, and feeling bandages around his head, he asked the nurse where he was.

"Am I at Riddle Memorial Hospital or Crozer-Chester Medical Center?"

The answer came in a dry emotionless business-like voice from the nurse.

"You're in a private institution, sir, as previously arranged."

Before he could ask another question, she abruptly left the room. As the door shut with a loud click, he noticed the reinforced wire mesh glass plate in the door's small viewing window. Looking again at the straps across his bed and the iron bars in the window, realizing the situation, he was in a mental institution somewhere, which was somehow, apparently, previously arranged. Thinking produced an instant throbbing headache, and movement caused surges of pain to rake across his entire body.

Dr. Winslow walked into his room with two ogres posing as orderlies followed by a dietitian; turns out the nurse had the best bed-side manner of the entire group. After looking at the charts at the end of the bed, Dr. Winslow moved to the side of the bed and spoke to John.

"Mr. Parella, you are quite lucky to have escaped such a fall without a serious internal injury."

"I feel like I was run over by a truck."

"You have extensive abrasions, contusions, a concussion, torn tendons around your ankle, and deep autumn bruises over most of your body."

"Autumn bruises? What the hell is that?"

"Sorry, it's a little joke the staff has — essentially, someone as bruised as you are will have red, brown and yellow splotches forming all over their body for weeks."

"Lucky me — do I get a prize?"

"You already won one: the fact that you were not killed, crippled, or seriously injured."

"Well, I still feel like crap. Any chance of getting a stronger painkiller?"

"Demerol is an opioid suitable for your level of pain; morphine is not warranted in your case. We will set you up with an automatic drip system for the next few days, and you can thumb press additional Demerol when you need it. It won't allow you to overdo it though."

"Not really needed? I feel like something stronger is needed."

"Mr. Parella, as I just said, nothing stronger is needed based on your injuries, and your records indicate a previous addiction to morphine."

"How the hell did you find that out? That is private, privileged information! How long have I been here?"

"You have been here four days in various states of consciousness. Records were made available to treat you. The MRI was good, showing no brain damage. Additionally, blood and urine samples indicate that no kidney, liver, or spleen damage is present. Your cholesterol and triglycerides are high though, and you are definitely overweight for your height. The dietitian had you on a maintenance caloric load while you were unconscious; she will continue that regimen, then take a complete diet history, and put you on a strict diet with solid foods while you're here."

"Where is here, and how long am I going to be here?"

"You are in a private institution."

Even though it was physically painful to get upset, John's frustration reached a pinnacle, and he started yelling.

"*What private institution am I in*? I keep asking but no one gives an exact answer! I never gave any personal or written instructions to anyone to put me in a private institution if I got hurt or sick, so who the hell authorized this?"

"Mr. Parella, if you do not calm down, we will sedate you; do I make myself clear?"

Exasperated, John said, "Yes, but please answer my questions."

"You will have to take up the matter of this choice of institution with your previous care provider; they have power of attorney when you are incapacitated."

"You mean the Clinic?"

"That is correct. In regards to how long you will be here, you will undergo physical therapy for your body; the state also requires a complete psychiatric evaluation to ensure that you are not a threat to yourself or anyone else. Miss Carnes will now take care of your dietary needs."

The two ogres stayed behind as well.

Chapter 6

AUDIENCE WITH THE KING

Islamic Year: 1377 AH   *1958 AD*

The King's vision for what Saudi Arabia was and what Saudi Arabia would become was taking shape. Though Saudi Arabia was younger in the development of oil fields as opposed to Iraq or Persia, its potential was phenomenal. In 1944, just over one hundred thousand barrels per day of oil was being processed. In 1953, Damman and Qatif had 36 producing wells, which together were processing one hundred thousand barrels a day, while the Abqaig and Ghawar fields together had 92 producing wells, with each site processing over four hundred thousand and three hundred thousand barrels a day, respectively. The stabilizer plants, which removed noxious and unusable gases from the crude oil were on-line and efficiently operating. And today, the three thousand square miles of *Rub al Khali*, meaning 'the Unknown Portion,' which is in the southern part of Saudi Arabia, was well into exploration and yielding positive results.[9]

Exploration crews had become self-sufficient; they had their own transport, living accommodations, food supplies, and means of communications with field operation headquarters.

Cable rigs were producing the needed water supplies from the Eocene and Miocene formations, and now the rail transport system was effectively linking all operations. In another decade, an order of magnitude increase in operational efficiency would be realized. This conquered kingdom of nomadic tribes was on the threshold of becoming a world power, yet they would do so without sacrificing their Muslim beliefs or cultural heritage. He would give his very life to ensure that was the case.[10]

The King, Crown Prince, princes, and members of the royal family made the train ride from Riyadh to Dammam. Eight private rail cars were set up to handle the royal family on this trip; three were for the private use of the royal family, three were assigned for meals, and two were used for receiving guests and select business partners. The Minister had arrived two days earlier to overview and approve all activities.

Dammam operations were now mature and mostly under Arab technical direction: the training classes, safety classes, rail car maintenance and drill rig maintenance classes were all lead by teams of trained Saudi instructors and workers. It was a pivotal moment to celebrate, one that the King and the Minister had been awaiting for many years. A band had been arranged to play as soon as the King arrived, with the Minister leading the band in his Rolls Royce.

John Parella, Sr. watched as the band assembled. Young boys with trombones, bass drums, and bag pipes, nervous and anxious to see the King, were all dressed in white pants and white shirts that flowed 10 inches below their waist. Each shirt was adorned with large brass buttons in the front, two on each sleeve, and a double row on the back; a black belt around the waist and grey berets on their head created the perfect balance of color. Soldiers marching behind the band wore the same beret on their head and had a similar mix of colors, except that their garb consisted of gray pants and a gray over-shirt that allowed the sleeves of a white undershirt to be seen on the full length of each arm. A white belt went around their waist, and a rifle was positioned perfectly on each of their right shoulders such that the barrel pointed straight up. It was quite impressive.[11]

After the parade, the King attended a live safety training class being conducted on gas-oil separators; he then attended an engine maintenance class on an oil rig, and observed a demonstration of how the 136 foot oil derricks are towed across the desert to their respective sites. At each session, he was very attentive and asked several safety questions as well as questions on operational costs and preventive maintenance. Everyone felt that he appreciated the importance of their role in Saudi Arabia's growth; however, when he came to inspect the trains and their maintenance schedules, he had an extra sparkle in his eyes. The King was enthralled by this technology. He climbed up ladders to look inside the engines used on the General Motors Locomotives that pulled all the freight cars, then spent an entire hour reviewing the various wheels, gear sets, and motor support journals used on the axles, asking probing questions on the relationships between rail type, load, and elasticity of the ballast and subsoil to support the rails.[12] At one point, the Minister had to politely remind the King of the other scheduled activities today, along with the early meetings back in Riyadh tomorrow morning. With a sigh, the King returned to the rail cars for the planned meal.

Mr. Jiling and John Parella, Sr. had been invited to eat in the first meal car with the King, the Crown Prince, the other princes, and the Minister. Tables three feet wide, covered in white linen, ran the full length of the rail car. Exquisite silverware and plain yet elegant China was at each place setting. Twelve stout wooden chairs lined each side of the table. Two armed guards were at each end of the rail car; Mr. Jiling and John sat at the far end of the table, right next to the armed guards closest to the exit. While the dinner conversation rarely involved Mr. Jiling or John, John noticed how they were being watched toward the end of the meal.

He had learned several things that were extremely insulting

to Arabs during his years in Saudi Arabia. The first was never to use the word *walad*, which means 'boy,' when speaking to a man.[13] Second, he painfully learned when you met an Arab, formalities were expected. The Minister had reinforced this expectation in their previous meeting. If someone greeted you by saying "peace be upon you (*as salaam 'alaikum*)," then the expected response was "and upon you (*wa 'alaikum as salaam*)." If a person asked, "How are you?," or "*Kaif Haalak?,*" then the expected response was "God be praised, very well," or "*Al Hamdu lillaah, Tayyib.*"[14] Third, never show the bottom of your shoe to anyone; this was synonymous with stating that you thought the person before you was no better than dirt. Fourth, never shake anyone's hand with your left hand, as this is the hand used to clean yourself after bowel movements, which was even a more egregious offense than showing someone the bottom of your shoe. Last, always belch after an Arab meal is served so that the host knows that you enjoyed the meal. Mr. Jiling was always apprehensive about this last custom; so, he let out a mild burp, which did raise an eyebrow or two along the table. John however was very confident in his response, letting out a loud belch that was greeted by smiles. Even the King was pleased.[15]

After dinner, the King requested Mr. Jiling and John to join him and the Minister in his private car for "Presentation of Gifts" and a brief discussion. The Minister presented ceremonial knives to Mr. Jiling and John for their diligent service over the last several years. Hand carved boxes, approximately twelve inches long lined with crushed felt, held each knife; the ivory handle was adorned with two rubies and one sapphire on each side. Both men were appreciative of the significance of the gift, thanking the Minister and the King. Each sincerely stated, in their own way, how honored they were to receive such a gift in recognition of their contributions.

The Minister proceeded to ask Mr. Jiling if he wouldn't mind sitting down and discussing the next rail car order, while he motioned them to move to the front of the King's private car.

The King proceeded to casually engage John in more technical questions about locomotive engines as they slowly moved to the rear of his rail car. The guards kept a cautious eye on everyone; a quick glance from the King signaled the guards to allow them the necessary space to talk in private. The King's private car had fewer windows than his other rail cars; so, it afforded space for personal adornments on the walls. Stopping at a picture of the Date Gardens at Hofuf, the King reminisced about the beauty of these gardens: how life managed to spring from rock and sand, how harsh and unforgiving desert life could be, and yet how many treasures, and not just oil, remained undiscovered, buried deep in the sands of his country.[16] John waited for the King to continue.

"Mr. Parella, you have spent several years of your life here, away from your family. You have two sons now, one of which is six years of age, and one that was just born, and you only see them, along with your wife a few weeks a year. How do you manage such a thing?"

"It is extremely difficult, but my wife and I are building a better life together for our family, and this makes the sacrifice worthwhile. She has saved nearly all the pay that I sent home, but I must admit that the strain of being away from my family has reached its limit."

"Yes, Mr. Jiling has told the Minister that you have submitted a letter of resignation and that you will continue to work for another ten months."

Looking down at the plush rug that he was standing on, John reflected on how incredible the opportunity was to work in Saudi Arabia. Here, you were rewarded for what you accomplished; not how old you were and how much seniority you had. Though there was plenty of work in the States, it was inhibited by seniority and union protocols; his ambition was suffocated in such a system. Interviewing twice for the job in New York, he was turned down the first time due to his age, but he was so persistent in subsequent months that he was granted a second interview. His drive, along with his knowledge of diesel mechanics learned in the Navy, proved to be a winning combination. Being the youngest person chosen for this work assignment, he didn't let anyone down; in fact, he exceeded all expectations and rose to the rank of Master Mechanic in a few years. Even now, he was reticent to give up this opportunity, but his wife was still living with his boys at her parents; it was time to get a place of their own. She needed his help raising the boys, and she was extremely lonely. John's parents were also pressuring him and his wife to end all this. It was time to go home.

John looked up sadly at the King. "I wish that I could stay longer. There is so much more to accomplish; here, life is pure, honest. The desert has become part of me."

With admiration, the King gazed into John's eyes. "You have helped Saudi Arabia a great deal and treated us with respect; we will honor your wishes, but I have another request to ask of you that will involve risk on your part. Based on your current situation, I would understand if you could not follow through on this request. It turns out that I will need your assistance in the previous matter that we discussed."

John took a deep breath; he was hoping that the King, with his vast resources, had found another solution to the dilemma that he now alluded to.

Mr. Jiling and the Minister were deep in conversation, as planned, but the King knew that he only had a few more minutes to explain everything before any suspicions were raised by Mr. Jiling, or the other dignitaries awaiting his audience that evening.

The King moved John over to a picture of a hilltop where thousands of Muslims were standing.

"This is the site of the Prophet Mohammed's last sermon in the plains of Arafat. It is part of the holy sites that Muslims see on the Hajj each year. Have you heard of the Hajj, and do you know its significance?"

Nodding his head, he had read up on this subject since many of his trainees had gone on the Hajj. The Hajj occurs on same six days of the lunar calendar each year. However, before the six days of the Hajj begins, pilgrims must first purify themselves fourteen days beforehand and recite the *talbiyah* to announce their intention to perform Hajj; this stage is called the Ihram or the purification. Next, before the Hajj begins is the Tawaf, where pilgrims walk counterclockwise seven times around the *Ka'bah*, center of Mosque in Makkah, to symbolize the central focus of Allah in their life. They then run between the hills of Safa and Marwah seven times to emulate the agonizing search for water by Abraham's wife, Hajar.[17]

The King was pleased to know that John knew of the religious significance of the Hajj. This made his task easier.

"It was on such a journey that my father discovered an unusual treasure in the desert, just at the turn of the century. He had a vision, which compelled him, after the Hajj, to return to the plains of Arafat and wander alone in the desert with one bodyguard for eleven days. He found scrolls written in Safaitic, Hismaic, and Greek, which are of some interest, but the most intriguing information was reflected in modern texts written in Arabic and Chinese. As incredible as it is to contemplate, this site was being maintained throughout the ages, by whom we have no idea, but the information had direct relevance on forming Saudi Arabia."

John was startled. "Are you saying that the information discovered helped your father and your family to unite the territories?"

"Yes, he was inspired to do so after reading and translating many of these texts, which discuss in great detail, all the possibilities in making certain decisions and the consequences associated with other decisions. Some of these texts actually reveal the future course of this world and Allah's plans for it, as well as plans for the Universe itself, which is all fascinating.

Other information speaks of advanced technologies that we never knew would exist, nor could we ever understand initially the purpose for why they were created. The totality of information is overwhelming, and the responsibility to govern this information is quite beyond one man's ability to do so."

John was puzzled. "Then why not share it with the world or simply destroy it?"

The King gritted his teeth, glowering for a second at John. Speaking in a low, stern voice, he said, "Mr. Parella, trust me when I say that the world is in no condition to digest or assimilate the ramifications of this information. The world squabbles over borders, currency, who practices the correct version of each religion, and whose religion is the purest message from Allah; do you really think that we are ready to embrace the master plan for this earth let alone the universe? And to even suggest thoughts of destroying information that surely comes from Allah himself would be blasphemy; my brother and I will not allow it."

Humbled, John stated, "Please forgive me; I was not completely thinking through the situation. I will certainly help in any way that I can, but I do not understand how I can be of help with such a task, given the vast resources that you command across the country."

The King clasped his hands behind his back, paused, and then spoke slowly. "Ah, now we reach the crux of the matter. In a few months, the King's absolute power to govern will be reduced; it is perhaps a necessary consequence of progress. Executive powers will be transferred to a prime minister and a cabinet will be formed later this year. And though the Royal family will still be very involved, more of the Royal family will need to be consulted in the decision making process. In addition, the individuals who know of this matter of course do not all agree on what should be done. I must act soon before I lose control of the situation. For my part in this, I have agreed to relinquish my rule to my brother several years from now;

publicly, a much more plausible explanation for the transfer of power will be presented to the world."

Looking straight at John, the King outlined part of his plan. "I will need you to provide a grand diversion, which some may even suspect to be a total farce; we only need to create a little uncertainty, and no one will really have the authority to stop anything as long as you can hold up under scrutiny. During the hot months when the work is very slow, the Minister will order tracks, freight cars, old rigging, and other scrap material to be buried in several desert sites around Dammam, Abqaig and Ghawar, as opposed to being salvaged: the reason being that current scrap metal prices would make such a decision somewhat plausible. However, the part that will raise suspicion is that, before the hot months, you will lay roughly one-third of the special track previously ordered at each of the three sites in succession."

"You remember that the Minister grilled you very thoroughly on this matter before. We are sorry that we had to cause you such personal stress at that time, but it was required in order to test you. The need to lay this track will be that the present crane that you have will have an accident that renders it completely unrepairable; therefore, one of the heavy duty cranes in Bahrain will have to be dismantled and brought down to Dammam. Suspicions will naturally arise because somehow this special track was fortuitously ordered ahead of time. You will dig each hole preciously at the location and to the dimensions dictated in the Minister's Order. Then you will dump the scrap into each hole, leaving this beacon device, encased in rubber to protect it, in one of the rail cars before you backfill each site."

"No one examining this device will understand how it really works. This particular positioning technology along with the power source to detect the beacon underground has not been fully developed yet. You will be watched very carefully; if anyone wants to inspect this device, the site, or orders you to wait several days to backfill any scrap sites, then you are to do so without raising any objections. You are to also answer any questions on the orders given to you. Just practice the answers that the Minister provided to you on all anticipated questions, and simply repeat the same answers over and over again. Even if you are asked a different question that was unanticipated, just use the answers provided. Your best personal protection in this matter is complete openness about what you are doing, and you must stick to the answers provided no matter how uncomfortable the questioning gets. Do you understand; can you accomplish this?"

"Yes, I understand. I know what to do."

"Very good, Mr. Parella. When all the sites are back-filled, you will receive an order, after the hot months, to remove the special track and store it as before, bulldoze the ballast and subsoil into the desert, and let nature and time work their magic. All this will afford me the time to do what I need to do. In parallel, you will train your replacement and then leave us during the first week of December."

"I will do as you request, but won't there be records and available transit coordinate readings of the exact locations of each scrap site?"

Amused, the King replied, "Yes. In fact, I am counting on this information being readily available to anyone who asks, and, to the few that know, we will even have the promise of more precise locations when the positioning technology is fully developed. This grand facade creates an impeccable diversion, while in the background keys critical to the future of the world are hidden. Now, let's return to Mr. Jiling and the Minister; we have conversed slightly longer than I had planned."

Chapter 7

THE PHONE CALLS

James Montgomery picked up the phone. As expected, it was Father Martin on the line.

"James, how are you? I am glad that I caught you and SuiLeng before your vacation. By any chance, did you happen to catch the news this morning?"

Sarcastically, James responded, "Which news would that be Father?"

Father Martin paused a moment; he had heard that sardonic, exasperated tone in James' voice before. This was the tone that always signaled a troubling moment for him.

"News from Pennsylvania: a second person has attempted suicide at the Clinic."

"Yeah, I just heard. You know —"

Father Martin cut off James' words before he could get them out.

"James, we discussed this the first time it happened, and now that it has happened again, it does not mean that you have to get involved."

"I thought that you preached getting involved when bad things happen in the neighborhood, Father."

Father Martin was getting perturbed. "Don't throw that back in my face; I am sure that your method of resolving this situation would be dramatically different than any solution that I would think of."

"So how much longer does this go on? Can't you see that he is never going to stop until I step into the arena?"

"James, this is not a boxing match. There are ways to handle this situation! Although I did not tell you this the first time, parties within the Church were notified when this happened before. This is not being swept under the rug as you might tend to believe; however, matters such as this take time to resolve. You have to be patient; you have a family now!"

James gritted his teeth, losing his cool. "Forgive my bluntness, but doling out penance is not going to solve this problem. It is time to act; I can't sit on the sidelines anymore! The reason that this is going to get resolved is exactly because I have a family now; we have a right to live life without fearing what might happen in the future or cringing with regret every time we ignore other victims that this maniac hurts to get to me. And I already told you before that if John Parella, Jr. was hurt, then I would be compelled to take action."

"SuiLeng lost one husband; do you want her to suffer through another loss like that?"

"Father, that fate will not be mine. If I have to, I will evolve further to resolve this. My family and I will not be the ones to suffer. I will ensure that."

Clearly shaken, Father Martin's voice trembled as he spoke. "James, you can't be serious; to choose that path could make you the animal that you always feared becoming. I would pray for your soul, but you have none. I will pray that your wife talks some sense into you."

James regretted talking this way to Father Martin, for he had steered James back onto the correct path more than once when James had lost his way. He owed Father Martin a lot—this was not the future that he envisioned just a few days ago, but his mind was made up. He would not allow any others to get hurt, and if anyone or anything so much as blinked the wrong way at SuiLeng or the boys, then he would exact immeasurable retribution.

"I have to go now; there are things to do."

With remorse in his voice, Father Martin tried one last time. "James, is there anything that I can say or anything that I can do that will change your mind? Or at least get you to delay your present course of action?"

"No, Father, there isn't."

"As soon as you leave Florida, you and your family will be hunted. That was the deal that we made. Is that what you really want?"

"No, it's not, but at least they will hunt me on my own terms in places that I choose to be. Goodbye, Father."

James hung up the phone. He decided to just sit in the kitchen and think until SuiLeng came down stairs; the conversation with his wife was going to be a hundred times more difficult than the one with Father Martin.

Sitting in the rectory chair with the phone pressed against his forehead, Father Martin felt a large migraine was on its way. He didn't have the strength to deal with the Bishop; the man needed such things explained to him twenty times over before he could grasp all the implications. There just wasn't time for that. Things would move fast now, and he would have to go on immediate leave, for personal reasons, in order to try and handle this himself. Up until now, his only concern on this situation was in Pennsylvania. Just what type of monster James might become was a whole new matter. Reminding himself that God never doled out challenges that you could not handle, he decided to have a private chat with the Big Boss tonight after night vespers to discuss the expectations on this one. Especially since he was thinking that his present skill set might be a bit inadequate to handle this situation.

Gemini Ascending

―――∞―――

As soon as Dr. Junger heard the news on the latest suicide attempt at his clinic, he politely excused himself mid-way through the conference and took the supersonic transport from Paris into the States. After clearing customs, his private driver picked him up and drove him back to his estate outside Toughkenamon, Pennsylvania. Everyone that came in contact with Dr. Junger on his return journey treated him as if he had just lost an immediate family member. Words were brief; farewell handshakes lasted a few seconds longer; the pats on the back and the expressions of concern were so sincere that he had to avert their gaze and bite his lower lip to keep from showing the elation that was welling up within him. If he didn't smile soon, he was going to burst.

Reflecting on the last forty three years of his present life, he noted the near demi-god status and the power that he wielded from a brilliant career. Being on the board of several health care institutions, he was consulted on candidates for key psychiatric positions across the country. In terms of his personal life, each of his three marriages had been delightful experiences. His wives were intelligent, career oriented, confident, and sexually vibrant. When the charm subsided and the conversations became inane regurgitations of daily life, each relationship ended amicably. There was a final hug, best wishes for one other, along with a sizable check, courtesy of a solid prenuptial agreement, plus the gift of a half case each of his spouse's favorite wines from what he was proud to say had to be one of the best wine cellars on the East Coast. In fact, after he freshened up, there were a couple of tri-blends that he had been saving for the last eight years. It was time to celebrate, for an irreversible set of events were now in motion.

There were a few reporters parked alongside the narrow country road that lead to his estate. His driver completely ignored the reporters; the guard opened the gate when his car arrived, and he was whisked across the eighty acres of land that lead to his fourteen room private mansion. His personal staff, consisting of two maids, a butler, a chef, a groundskeeper, and several security guards, was at the front door waiting for him. Before exiting the car, he decided to make his staff wait longer as he made a phone call; he would shortly put on a dour complexion and grille each staff member on what had been accomplished during his absence. However, he was in such a good mood that he had to share it with someone; perhaps James Montgomery felt like talking.

Dr. Junger dialed the Florida number and waited for someone to answer. After four rings he hung up and wondered if the newlyweds were still in bed. Maybe as a courtesy he should let them sleep, but what if they haven't heard the news yet? It would be exquisite if he was the first one to tell them what had happened; he dialed again.

James Montgomery looked up at the phone when it first rang. It stopped ringing right before he could decide what to do. Although the news would be troubling to her, he wanted to talk to SuiLeng before taking any more phone calls, because she had an analytic, insightful nature. When the phone rang again, James hesitantly picked up the receiver.

"Hello, this is James Montgomery."

"James, good morning. This is your dear old friend, Dr. Junger. I hear that congratulations are in order; you were just married yesterday weren't you?"

James breathed in and out several times without answering.

"James, you sound out of breath. I suppose marriage can do that to you. You know I had three wonderful marriages; each one was a unique experience that lasted for many years. You know, the best advice that I can give is that you have to work at marriages. The honeymoons are nice, but the secret is to continue to talk to one another and share life's dreams and experiences — be true partners."

Feed up with the banter, James responded, "Great advice

Doctor. So, why couldn't you make one marriage last? Did the commitment to one woman get to be too much for you?"

"James, how could you suggest such a thing? I deeply loved all my wives; we simply realized that we could no longer grow together. Each party knew when the time had come to exit the relationship. All my relationships ended pleasantly with no animosity, which is the true sign of mature, consensual relationships."

"Sounds to me like the prenuptial agreements were coming close to termination. You always were one to keep your hard earned possessions close to the vest, eh, Dr. Junger?"

"James, such a personal attack is unbecoming of you. It demeans your true nature. Here I am trying to congratulate you on your very first marriage to a wonderful woman with two handsome and energetic young boys and all you can do is grouse over my three previous marriages. Perhaps I should not have called you today."

James eyes glowed with rage. "Personally, I would like it if you never called, talked to, or interacted with me again in my entire lifetime."

"Now, James, that would be a very long time indeed, and we have shared so many private moments during your life that I could not imagine never being in contact with you again. It is unthinkable. *I even named a hotel after you.*"

"Dr. Junger, I am not your friend, nor will I ever be your friend. I have no respect for you or any of your work, especially your work of late, and naming a hotel after me, under the circumstances, just shows how twisted your mind really is."

"Every leading edge scientist has a few setbacks. Einstein knew his theory of relativity to be a breakthrough even though it would be years before it could actually be proven."

"Einstein didn't screw up people's lives."

"On the contrary, James, he had to spend so much time thinking alone that he distanced himself from his first wife and family. They were distracting him from his work. These are the sacrifices that need to be made to move the world forward, and it takes very strong men to make such decisions. Now, I must admit that I have misjudged some of my staff's ability to handle certain matters at the Clinic, but I will correct that situation shortly."

James sternly replied, "So you are going to destroy more people's lives as they take the blame for your misguided forays into the human mind?"

Dr. Junger laughed. "James, science must progress."

"I am not going to play your game."

With a lecturing, fatherly voice, Dr. Junger stated, "Now, you don't really mean that. I know you too well. It's just that you are a little unsure of yourself right now, and things are confusing. Being married, having two sons to raise, these are big responsibilities for one such as yourself, and God only knows what kind of spiritual tenets that priest, Father Martin, has filled your head with. You know, James, you don't do too well with the different religions in the world. You really did much better when you were an American Indian. In fact, I would advise you to think back to those days of your previous life and the other woman that you once married who was your so-called 'soul mate.' Have you told SuiLeng about her yet?

Standing up, James raised his voice. *"You sick bastard! How dare you even talk about her! You damn well know why we were never married!"*

"Okay James, whatever you say. See you soon, and have a nice day." With that Dr. Junger hung up the phone.

James was still standing up in the kitchen with the phone in his hand when he noticed SuiLeng and the boys staring at him off to the side in the family room.

Chapter 8

THE FIRST SESSION

Dr. Duhring was standing behind her desk glancing over her notes, waiting for her 9 AM appointment, when Bill Eckland knocked on her door.

"Hello, Bill; how are you doing today? How's the family?"

"Doing well, thank you Doctor. I was wondering if you had a few minutes."

"Yes, we can chat until my 9 o'clock gets here."

"Well, your 9 o'clock is what I wanted to chat with you about."

"Really?" A pause. "Well, sit down. Let's hear it."

"Well, I probably should have brought this to your attention before, but it was so strange that I had to process it a while before mentioning it to you. When we were bringing Mr. Parella in from Chadds Ford, he was delirious, slipping in and out of consciousness the whole way in. I think that he thought that I was his mother at one point, but that aside, the voices that he used the rest of the time really shook Stan and I up."

"Voices, what do you mean?"

"Well, it was like he was four different people; he had his

normal voice, then he started talking like he was someone else, and the woman's voice really floored us."

"Bill, do you mean he acted a bit psychotic? That is common for the trauma that he suffered; even schizophrenic behavior has been documented in such cases; you've seen this before."

"Yes, I know, I have seen that before, but this was different. He wasn't just mimicking other personalities with his voice; his voice was other people. It was totally different in pitch and tone. It really freaked us out. If you closed your eyes and listened, you would have thought that three other people were back there carrying on a conversation with him."

Dr. Duhring took a moment to digest this information. If it was any other person from the EMS team other than Bill Eckland, she would have thought that this was just another prank being played on the newest female member of the staff. But in the last eighteen months that she had been on staff here, Bill's on-scene diagnostics, maturity, and decisiveness in handling patients had earned her respect.

"Alright, Bill, I'll take this under advisement; thanks for bringing it to my attention."

On his way out of her office, Bill paused at the door. "Be careful with this one, Doctor."

Seeing the concern in Bill's face made her reevaluate the situation. Perhaps there was more to this than the present set of facts revealed. She had read all the case files from the Clinic and had also stopped at the library and pulled up several microfiche articles from the various magazines and local newspapers that documented Mr. Parella's accomplishments, success, and demise. She was reviewing her notes for the initial meeting when Mr. Parella arrived in his wheelchair with the orderlies.

"Doctor, your 9 o'clock is here. Would you like us to stay?"

"Yes, I think that would be a good idea."

Evan and Stephen, the two orderlies that John had referred to as 'ogres' left John in his wheelchair in front of Dr. Duhring and took seats on the other side of the office.

"Great, are Fric and Frac going to sit through all our sessions together?" quipped John.

"Mr. Parella, their names, as displayed on their badges, are Evan and Stephen. And to answer your question, until I establish what your mental condition is, it is the policy of this institution to have orderlies present in all sessions. Shall we begin now?"

John sighed while looking around the eclectic office surrounding him. Dr. Duhring's mahogany desk was dark, cold, and very clean, with just a few papers on it. A coffee pot, a few handmade coffee mugs, and family pictures sat on the credenza on the right side of the room. Fric and Frac were sitting in wicker chairs on the far left end of the room underneath several diplomas mounted on the wall. Being near sighted, John could not make out all the institutions on the various degrees, but he was sure that she had impeccable credentials; her office door stated that she was the Director of Psychiatry. Looking back toward Dr. Duhring, the three tall arched wire mesh windows behind her were bordered with embossed green wallpaper creating the perfect institutional peace-de-résistance.

"Mr. Parella, you drifted off — would you like to begin the session now?"

Looking at the floor, John answered, "Yes."

Still sitting behind her desk near the windows, she replied, "Mr. Parella, I am over here."

Shifting his gaze toward the Doctor, he noticed how gorgeous she was.

"You're getting distracted again."

Slightly blushing, yet forming a little smile, John looked at her face and stammered, "I'm sorry, I was just, ah, just...you know...well, to be truthful, just kind of admiring your beauty."

"Yes, I could see that, can we begin now please?"

With her raised eyebrows, wrinkled forehead, and pursed lips surrounded by flowing strawberry blonde hair, John made a mental note of just how beautiful she really was. He also thought about how hard it was for women to make it in the workplace; he had seen that in his own company. If a woman was intelligent, but not tough enough, then none of the men would listen to her. If she was intelligent and tough, then the men labeled her a 'bitch.' And if she was intelligent, tough, and had great leadership and team building skills, then the other women in the office would undermine her out of jealousy. A successful woman in the workplace was basically alone. He had to admire the woman in front of him; she would have to be something special to overcome the incredible pressure and office politics to be here; and she would have to possess a very healthy dose of self-confidence.

In a chastising tone, Dr. Duhring spoke again, "Mr. Parella, you are clearly having trouble concentrating today; so, I think that it would be best to try our first session again tomorrow."

Surprised, John shook away his thoughts and replied, "Tomorrow, why?"

"These sessions will be mentally challenging; it will require some diligence on your part to get through them, which is why they have been scheduled every morning at this time. However, if at any time you are not ready for a session, then we will simply postpone it to the next day."

Whining a bit, John asked if they could just meet in the afternoon.

"In the afternoon, if you'll remember, you have extensive physical therapy after which you will be quite exhausted; this would not be conducive to the sessions that I have in mind. Stephen, Evan, please escort Mr. Parella back to his room; we will try again tomorrow."

Noting that everyone had a smile on their face except him, John mumbled a few sentences to himself as Fric and Frac lead him out of the doctor's office. As they proceeded down the hallway, he commented on the institution's lack of color coordination.

"My goodness, is there no other color than white in this place? The ceiling panels are white, the walls are white, the doors are white, the baseboard is white, the floor tiles are white with just a few specks of gold in them, and even the non-stainless steel parts of my wheelchair are white. I feel like I'm in a blizzard. No wonder patients get disoriented around here when they enter an office with some color in it; they suffer from mental white-out the rest of the time."

"Actually, there are over 170 variations of white commercially available; it just so happens that this is the most soothing color of white that there is," Fric stated.

John responded, "You're kidding right? Did you write a dissertation on this?"

"No, I worked in a paint store. You would be amazed at how many people cannot put any other color than shades of white in their house."

"Oh, so working in a paint store is a prerequisite for a job like this? You must have lifted a lot of paint cans to get a body like that."

John then turned his attention to Frac. "So, what's your story? You work in the same paint store?"

Smiling, Evan spoke. "No, I had a much harder life. I worked in a supermarket before this job; you know the unpack and stack shift from midnight to 8 AM every day."

Stephen started laughing.

"Alright, you guys are having fun with me. Fine, look, I'm sorry that I called you Fric and Frac; I'm just really pissed off right now. I was hoping to get some help, and here I am in a place that apparently has no name, with people that I don't even know who sure know a lot about me. I hope that you can understand why I am bit irritated over this whole thing."

Evan answered in a sympathetic voice, "Mr. Parella, I can assure you that the staff here is extremely competent; Stephen and I have seen miracles worked here in very short order. When cases like yours come along, two orderlies are assigned to be with the patient twenty-four hours a day. Both Stephen and I have two year degrees, and, as you might guess, have black belts in different martial arts. We can pretty much handle anything that might arise as a first line response team."

"That sounds very expensive, who the heck is paying for all this? No wonder state taxes keep going up."

"Well, actually, you are paying for all this while you're here, as stipulated in your primary care giver agreement," Stephen replied. "This is not really a state run institution; sure, the state has guidelines that must be followed, but, as a private institution, the facility has leeway for patient care that state run institutions cannot afford."

"Really?" John was curious now. "So, just what kind of leeway are you talking about?"

A little nervous, Stephen mumbled his next set of words, "Well, you aren't supposed to find out about this until you have been a little more cooperative, but you can pretty much go anywhere on the grounds after your therapy and rehab sessions up until 6 PM, as long as Stephen and I are with you. That would include the library, the pool, the movie theatre, the exercise facilities, etc. In fact, in a case like yours, more interaction is actually encouraged."

John was astounded. "Are you shittin' me? This sounds like Club Med, not a mental institution! But what the hell happens after 6 PM?"

"No, we're not kidding you, Mr. Parella," replied Evan. "This institution is paid for by its clients, as we like to call them, which is why we refer to all sessions as appointments. This conveys mutual respect for the people who pay the bills. Now, as for 6 PM, that is when Stephen and I have to split apart. One of us goes to sleep while the other one takes the 6 PM to 1 AM shift, watching you outside your room. At 1 AM, we switch and that person watches you from 1 AM to 8 AM while the other person sleeps."

"You mean to tell me that you guys work seventeen hours a day and sleep for seven? Criminy, you guys must love your work."

"We actually love the pay; working here for six month rotations is equivalent to working a full year somewhere else. It allows us to engage in other entrepreneurial pursuits the rest of the year," Evan piped in.

John was impressed. "Oh, I am not even going to ask what those other interests are. So do you get a choice in who you are assigned to?"

"Not usually, but in your case, we did ask to be assigned to you. We thought that we would be able to learn some things from you after we got to know you," Stephen answered.

"What the hell are you guys going to learn from me? I blew my business, my marriage, my relationship with my kids, my relationships with all my friends, I don't even like myself anymore, and I can't even commit suicide properly."

"Mr. Parella, everyone has ups and downs in life. If you had really wanted to kill yourself, you would have chosen a more effective method. I suspect that you just need someone to help you get back on your feet."

"Christ, that sounds good. Can you be my Doctor?"

"No, but we can take you down to the cafeteria to see if any of those breakfast rolls are still left, then show you around the place."

Feeling the first bit of cheer in his new place of residence, John responded, "Well, as Humphrey Bogart said in Casablanca, this could be the beginning of a beautiful relationship, boys. Now, let's see about those breakfast rolls."

"Let's not get carried away, Mr. Parella."

"Okay, okay, I was just pushing the envelope a little to see where the boundaries were; that's the first rule of business you know."

John's first rehab session that afternoon only lasted one hour; he was so out of shape that he could only do light stretches in the pool followed by a pitiful set of laps with a lot of rest in between sets. His rehab instructor, who looked like an Olympic swimmer, had no compassion. At the end of the session, John was curtly told that the sessions would work up to three hours in totality. When he was in better shape, he would do much more extensive pool work, followed by weight training, and finish up with yoga. John later learned that this particular health care professional just loved pool work because it keep the weight off of joints initially, and allowed the heart rate to stay lower; therefore, he could push his patients harder, which often lead to faster recovery periods. Eating dinner at 5 PM, John was brought to his room by 6 PM. Being so tired, his bed felt like a plush bed at a Westin Hotel; at 6:08 PM, he slept like a baby through the night.

The following morning, Stephen and Evan helped him shower and dress, get to breakfast at 8:30 AM and be back in Dr. Duhring's office at 9 AM.

Dr. Duhring was sitting at her desk as John was wheeled into her office. She noticed that he looked more chipper today than yesterday. "Well, Mr. Parella, you look like you had a good night's sleep; are you ready for your session today?"

"Absolutely, Doc. Stephen and Evan had me up and at 'em early this morning—we are all set to go."

"Please refer to me as Doctor Duhring. Likewise, I am glad to see that you are using Stephen and Evan's proper names."

"Oh, we're cool. We had a great day yesterday getting to know each other; they thought of a great nickname for me."

Dr. Duhring looked over at the orderlies and saw that they were smiling and nodding their heads. She was always amazed at men; they were insensitive, piggish, and downright slobs at times, yet they made friends quickly. They would support and forgive one another so easily that it made her envious at times. They could make decisions without all the facts, yet they never regretted wrong decisions or even felt badly about them, and they could commit to a project deadline without a clue as to how they were going to get it done. If only women could band together like men did and not be so self-conscious about being wrong or just winging it, and if they could just support one another, then they might even take over the world. Maybe twenty years from now things will be different.

Dr. Duhring started the session. "Well, let's save the nickname for later Mr. Parella. Now, let's start with what was going on the day that you jumped off the wall at the Clinic. What were you thinking about?"

"Well, I was thinking that I had to get away. I felt trapped and depressed; I needed a change."

"You signed yourself into the Clinic; you could have left at any time. Why did you need to make such a statement? What did you hope to accomplish?"

John looked away. "Boy, you don't ease into a subject, do you? Look, it's kind of complicated. I needed to get away, and that was the best way I could think of at the time."

Dr. Duhring mulled this over for a second before responding. "Was this an impulsive decision on your part, or had you planned this for a while?"

John hesitated. "Actually, it was...well, I have been thinking about it for a while. I was having dreams and things for some time, and these things sort of just sent me in a certain direction."

"What things besides dreams, Mr. Parella?"

John clenched his jaw before speaking, "Let's just leave it at *things* for now, Dr. Duhring."

"Did you ever mention any of this to anyone at the Clinic in your sessions there?"

"I am sure that you know the answer to that question already. You probably have already reviewed the taped sessions that I had there the last several months."

"Actually, I listened to all the sessions that you had over the last six months, and, although it seemed that you were not making much progress over that time, there was nothing that I detected that would lead me to believe that you were contemplating suicide. So what were you holding back in your sessions? What things came up, and what were your dreams about?"

– 57 –

"Well there were several dreams about my father; he passed away a few years ago. And there were other dreams."

"Go on, Mr. Parella, what happened in the dreams?"

John sighed. "Well the dreams about my Dad were mostly fond memories of us doing stuff together: fishing, working on construction jobs in the summer, things like that. But then they got weird. Almost all the dreams and things that I had over the last month were weird."

"Which parts were weird?"

"The part where they advised me to hurt myself...to attempt suicide in the exact manner that I did in order to start a new life," John answered softly, looking back down at the ground.

"I see. Well, tell me about your father; what kind of relationship did you have with him? What did you love about him? Did he ever make you mad? Did you respect him? What do you regret from his death?"

"Oh, I loved my Dad a lot. I loved his honesty, his strength, his generosity. He worked hard, and he was strong, decisive, well read and analytical; he knew several trades, and he enjoyed life and talking to people. I just really regret not being able to spend more time with him."

"What are the fondest memories of your Dad over the years—memories between just you and him?"

"You're getting personal now, Doc."

"Dr. Duhring, Mr. Parella."

John sighed again. "Alright, Dr. Duhring it is. One moment that pops to mind was when I was eleven. I had gotten straight A's on my report card. My dad was very proud of me; he came in my room and gave me a kiss—a short peck on the lips, and said that true men can show their pride and respect for one another in such a gesture. Then he made a joke by saying that the French can only manage to kiss each other on the checks, but Italians are blessed; so, they can express their love and pride in many ways."

"Another private moment that I remember was when I was

sixteen; my dad and I were breaking up a concrete walkway. He asked me to hold the three foot steel chisel while he hit the top end or head with an eight pound sledge hammer. I was really nervous, afraid that he would miss and break my wrist or my arm. He told me that he never missed when a man was holding the chisel. Until that moment, he hadn't ever called me a man before; in total trust, I put both hands on the chisel and held it firm. Each time I reset the chisel, he tapped the head with two half-strokes to get his rhythm, then he let loose with full swings until the chisel broke through the concrete. I was so amazed at the accuracy and raw power of each strike. I will never forget that."

"Later on, another special moment was after graduating from college. We went night fishing off the ice breakers in the Delaware Bay, and the ocean was so smooth. A full moon was out; we didn't catch a thing, and we hardly said a word all night, but the time together was beautiful. It had such an effect on me that I had to write a poem about it."

"Yes, I have read your book of poems. They cover quite a range of subjects. Before I inquire about them though, tell me something about your dad that you were not happy or proud of."

"Well, Dr. Duhring, there was just one thing: both he and my mom could never tell one another just how much they truly loved each other. Each of them would tell my brother and I how much they loved the other person, and how much they missed each other when they were apart, but we were not allowed to pass this information on. They were both so strong in their personalities that each one was afraid that the other person would take advantage of them if they acknowledged how much they loved each other. As strong as my dad was mentally and physically, this insecurity was the only weakness that he had."

"Did your dad and mom ever fight?"

"Are you kidding me? They were one hundred percent Italian! They fought like two rams on a steep hilltop; neither one would give an inch. They could argue about the color of toilet paper that went into their bathroom for hours; then they would make-up, kiss and hug with loving affection. Sometimes, I would laugh at the relationship that they had; most times though, I would just shake my head. I knew that they loved one another, but two thoroughbreds of the same nationality in the same house was tough sometimes. So, I decided that I would not marry an Italian girl, because we would probably kill each other."

"That's an interesting decision, when did you tell your parents about that one?" Doctor Duhring raised her eyebrows.

"I didn't have to tell them; they noticed by the time that I was seventeen that I never dated an Italian girl. So one day, my mom confronted me in the kitchen on the subject. I didn't have the heart to tell her that I did not want a life where my wife and I fought like cats and dogs on everything, that it would be best to marry someone that did not have the same temperament as me. So I told her that Italian girls came in two varieties, and I could not marry either one. This peaked her curiosity; so, she asked me to explain what I meant. I told her that Italian girls were usually always beautiful and great kissers, which she agreed with. I proceeded to tell her that type one of Italian girls are lazy, and they just want to stay home, be pampered by their husband while he works, and sleep in every day, and that I couldn't marry a girl like that. The other type of Italian woman is a workaholic, who works a full time job plus takes care of the house, and the house has to be spotless. They are loud, and they nagged you until your ears fell off."

"Then she asked me what type she was. After I pointed out to her that she worked a full time job, that we always had to take our shoes off at the front door, that the floor was so clean that you could eat off of it, and that she always told us what she was concerned about at least ten times over as loud as she could, she realized that she was type two. At which point, she threw a wet kitchen rag at my head. However, that little talk never deterred her from constantly having her Italian work friends conveniently stop by on Sundays with their daughters.

I must admit that I was really tempted to date some of them, but I knew after the first kiss that it would be too hard to get away."

"Tell me about your mom, Mr. Parella."

"She is 120 pounds of tough love; we had to do our chores each week around the house, help our dad on the weekend with jobs that he contracted, and we had to get top grades in school, or we never heard the end of it. She believed that a hard work ethic combined with a good education was the key to success. I think that she was right about that. She also fervently protected us—whether we were right or wrong. Whenever we got into a street fight, or had difficulties with a classmate or a disciplinarian at any school, she came to our rescue when she deemed things had gone too far. I loved her for her fearlessness to take anyone on. In essence, she was the only one allowed to discipline us. She had a soft side too; I could tease her about her personality and the crazy things that went on at her job, and she would laugh so heartily that I would laugh with her."

In an inquisitive tone, Dr. Duhring asked what compelled John to write the poems that he wrote, noting that he wrote about lost childhood moments, death and the longing and purity of love.

John thought about this for a few seconds before answering. "I write mostly when I am sad or very introspective. In terms of the words themselves, I feel that poetry shouldn't lecture; it should flow tastefully, be a pleasure to the ear and yet leave the reader with a powerful thought. Some of my poems have taken close to a year to get just right."

Dr. Duhring was gaining an insight into John. He was not a spoiled, rich, intelligent brat who had everything handed to him. From the articles that she read, his parents had created considerable wealth with honest, hard work. Apparently, he was also expected to work right along with them plus hit the books the rest of the time, which he did with great success.

"Did school work come easy to you? Were you one of those people who had to study one hour a night to get straight A's in all subjects?"

John grunted, "Hell no, my brother was the smart one in the family; nothing came easy to me. I had to work at Math, English, and Science. It took me three plus hours a night of studying on school nights plus studying all Sunday afternoon to get and maintain the grades that I got. However, working this hard was what I was used to, so high school and college were challenging but not impossible to get through. Plus, at that point in my life, I never gave up even when I got a failing grade on a test—it just motivated me to try harder."

"When did you lose that attitude in your life, Mr. Parella?"

"I guess the downward slide started after screwing my colleagues and close personal friends out of millions of dollars. Before that, my marriage and my relationship with my kids had already failed by spending so much time at work to build up my company. That's when I checked myself into the Clinic for the first time. Then my dad passed away later, and I completely stopped caring after that."

Dr. Duhring looked at John and noted that he was getting pensive. Having a great deal of information to review from this session, she asked John if he would like to end the session today and continue again tomorrow. John was grateful for a choice. Initially energetic, he now felt drained, and he wanted some fresh air. Perhaps he could convince Evan and Stephen to take him on another tour of the grounds followed by another breakfast roll. Unfortunately, the dietitian had caught him in the cafeteria yesterday; she noted what he was eating and removed his dessert from dinner. The 1500 calorie a day diet along with boot camp in the afternoon and mental probing in the morning was either going to cure him or kill him; there was no middle ground allowed at this institution.

Chapter 9

BREAKFAST

SuiLeng walked slowly and deliberately into the kitchen with her arms folded over her bathrobe; the children following cautiously.

Speaking in a curt manner, SuiLeng asked, "James Montgomery, who the hell was that on the phone, and why were you and Father Martin arguing; what is going on?"

In a low exasperated voice, James said, "Let's eat breakfast then talk; I was going to make homemade pancakes."

Staring firmly back at James, "No, we are going to talk now! You boys go watch TV."

Looking at one another, the boys got nervous. Their mother hated TV; she always ranted about what a total waste of time it was. Cautiously, Chun Soon, or CS, asked if they were still going on vacation to Disney World in Orlando.

"Yes, now, go watch TV," she responded, irritated.

The boys didn't need to be told twice; they normally had to beg for days to watch TV. With their vacation fears alleviated, they practically ran into the family room. Besides, James looked like he could handle himself; however, when PeoBing, or PB, turned around, he saw that his mother had grabbed James' hand and was leading him upstairs. He thought that maybe James was going to need some help after all.

After James walked into their bedroom, SuiLeng closed the door behind her and stood there waiting for an explanation. Watching her stand there with her arms folded tightly across her chest made him a bit nervous. Even though he had engaged in fierce battles before, he never remembered his stomach being so squeamish.

"Well, are you going to say something, James?"

In a very low voice, James uttered, "Yes, we need to talk about some things in my past life."

"Which life are we speaking of, the one with the person that you called a bastard, the one with Father Martin, or the one where you were married before?"

"SuiLeng, I was never actually married before, well, I almost was."

"Why have you never told me about this before?"

James looked up and when he spoke, there was some anger in his voice. "I did tell you about her; remember the story about Sunflower, and how much I loved her. I just decided to leave a few pieces out. They are painful memories."

SuiLeng didn't back down; matching the tone of his voice and raising hers a bit, she strongly suggested that he tell her the whole story this time around and then she would judge if it was appropriate to have left out the parts that he did.

"After I was brought into the tribe, I hunted, tilled crops tirelessly, and fought enemies of the tribe, yet many tribe members were still reluctant to fully accept me because I showed no interest in any of the women. Finally, my adopted grandmother changed her mind and thought it would be best for me to take a wife; she thought that it would fully integrate me into the tribe's daily life, and it would end the constant ogling from the young women in the village, giving the other men a chance to take a wife."

Not amused at the beginning of this story, SuiLeng blurted out, "So, you were quite a stud back then."

Ignoring this, James continued. "But my grandmother thought that it would be prudent to let it be known that I was sterile so as not to mislead the young women in the village. In her healing classes, she was able to carefully divulge that I was interested in taking a wife but that a hunting accident had left me with the strong possibility that I would never father children. This information caused many of the young women to become disinterested in me."

"Oh, that must have hurt your sex life."

"SuiLeng, please, let me at least tell the story."

"Go on, James, I haven't heard anything yet that has helped the situation."

"Well only one woman in the tribe was still interested, and that was Sunflower. As I told you before, we spent time together over many months; I followed out the tribe's customs to the letter, and I fell deeply in love with her as I told you before."

"Yes, you told me all this before. So why couldn't you tell me that you intended to marry her? Why did you have to hide that?"

"Because she was viciously murdered before we were married. Because I love you as deeply and passionately as I loved her. Because I have no religion to bolster my strength; I have no God to pray to. I only have fate, and I was so afraid that the same thing would happen to you, to us, before we were married such that I could not mention it. I was too scared."

Seeing the pain in his face, SuiLeng came over to James and held him. "You still could have told me."

"I want to tell you how she died."

SuiLeng looked up at him; they moved toward the bed, sitting down beside each other. "Then tell me."

"Sunflower and I would take deep walks into the woods. Sometimes it would be for a day, but on other occasions, we would travel and camp for weeks, living off the land. At times, we would end up near the foreigner's villages. Back then, along the Chesapeake and Delaware Bay, which were not even referred to as colonies yet, people lived and shared the land; it was a beautiful time, but there were always bad people. Some of the traders saw Sunflower and wanted me to barter her to them even after I told them that we were to marry. Although this had been done with honor with a few women in the village, I could tell that these men had no real interest in raising families. They wanted Sunflower for lustful reasons only; so, I continued to refuse their offers. I was very wary on the way back to the village; I knew that they were following us, but they eventually traded their goods and left; or so I thought. After I returned from a hunting party, Sunflower was found ravaged and beaten. She was barely alive when I reached her and my grandmother; her internal wounds were too severe to heal. When I held her in my arms, she was too weak to speak, but I smelled the men who had done this to her. When I looked into her eyes, I saw what had happened. I saw how bravely she fought off the three men who ravaged her. I saw how she struggled against them even as they beat her and held her down. I heard her call for my name over and over again; she was pleading for help, pleading for them to stop. Then, I heard her whisper her love for me just before she passed out from the pain. The last bit of sparkle in her eyes told me that she knew I could read her mind. I was able to tell her how much I loved her and share what I knew of myself with her. She died late in the night with one last look at me while holding her father's and mother's hands, who were on either side of her."

"My adopted grandmother, adopted father, and several Indians were outside the teepee, crying as I passed by them. Striding to the central village fire, I knelt, and melted crystals from my pouch, letting them burn both my hands and face when I smeared them on. The pain focused me. Standing up, pulling my knife from its sheath, I let loose endless screams of pain and anguish, screaming at the sky, at the moon, screaming for revenge, screaming with such heart rendering force that the crickets stopped chirping and the wolves stopped howling for hours after I left."

"Running all night and into the next day, I found them at last; they received no mercy at all from me. Inflicting physical and mental pain, I carved the weapons out of their hands, broke their bones, crushed their bodies and scalped them alive to show my disrespect. Then I watched them die. Returning their scalps to the village, I said good-bye that very day to my adopted grandmother and father. We all knew that my days as an animal had begun; I had never killed for revenge before. After that, I decided to enter the white man's world. I would learn their ways, try to understand how they thought, and I vowed to kill them all if they were evil."

"From Sunflower's death came two revelations about myself. I can enter another person's mind when they are suffering terrible duress and are in a state of shock, very close to death. I was able to bring some peace to Sunflower before she died. In the three men that I killed, I was also able to implant a picture of the fire that I saw from my birth before their death. I enjoyed watching them think that a lifetime of damnation awaited them when they finally left this world. To this day, I feel absolutely no remorse over any of these actions. The second thing that I learned was how easily I can change my skin color when I put my mind to it."

Hesitating before speaking, SuiLeng said, "I forgive you for not telling me all about her before. While such events in your past have shaped the being that you are, bitter, agonizing memories like these are best left alone. I also sense that you were afraid to tell me this for how I might react to how you killed the men who harmed your previous wife. You should feel no shame; my family would have done the same."

"She was not—"

SuiLeng put her finger on James' mouth. "Shhh, my love. Let me talk. She was, in essence, your wife to be; you loved her with the passion and commitment that you love me. To hear you speak of love in such terms and to know that in all your lifetimes you have only found two women to share such love with makes my heart melt. I love you so much; promise me that you will try to share more of your past lives with me. I know it's hard, having lived so long, but try and pick out the things important to me, to us, to our family. Now, is this changing skin color bullshit, or can you really do it?"

Standing up, letting his robe drop to the floor, he matched his skin tone to her's. Speechless for just a second, she let her robe fall down around her. Moving close to James, stroking his inner thigh, she whispered in his left ear, "I've always wanted a Chinese man as strong and firm as you are; make love to me."

"But I thought that you still wanted to know about all the phone calls," James playfully responded.

"After breakfast, James, after breakfast."

When SuiLeng and James came downstairs, they were arm in arm, and they had that look again in their eyes like they had for the last month before they were married. The boys were hoping that it would have taken a bit longer to resolve the issue, whatever it was; they were getting into some serious mind-numbing cartoon entertainment, which would end as soon as Mom saw what they were watching. It was good to see their mom happy again though, smiling like she used to when their real father was alive, and, while she was still tough as nails on discipline, they noticed that James was able to convince her to mitigate their punishments to half sentences and sometimes even quarter sentences, which was cool. James himself was physically much stronger than their father, but he was a lot like their dad in other ways: letting them be silly and burn off the crazy energy that all boys have, and watching cartoons with them when Mom wasn't around, which really made her mad. On the other hand, he could be serious, teaching them things they were curious about: like how a car's engine worked, how lightening is created, and how to perform martial art moves without falling down. In fact, he could answer any question they asked, although he was a real pain in the neck when he thought that you didn't understand enough of the basics. Mom summed it up best when she said that James would never just give you a simple answer to your question; he had to go back to the beginning of time to explain all relative information so that he was sure you understood the answer he was giving you. The boys knew that their mom loved James, and, while they would always love their father their entire lives and have fond memories of him, James was part of their new family, and they were finding room in their hearts for him.

SuiLeng finally noticed what the boys were watching on TV.

"What is that garbage that you two are watching? Shut that off and get over here for breakfast, and after that I don't even want to hear any whining about watching TV for another month. We have a plane to catch, and I expect you to help pack. You boys are old enough now to start helping more around the house and on trips, and I want those rooms cleaned before we—."

Before SuiLeng could say anymore, James had stuffed a dollar pancake in her mouth and had followed that up with a kiss.

As the boys got up to turn the TV off, they looked at one another and nodded. Yep, it was sure good to have James in their lives.

Chapter 10

DR. JUNGER RETURNS

Dr. Adolphus Junger awoke at 4 AM that Monday morning, on what would become another beautiful May day, so refreshed and full of cheer that he almost contemplated taking the day off and doing some serious reading out in the gardens. But there was so much more fun to be had at the office today. Completely disrupting his secretary's weekend by calling her at 7 AM on Saturday morning, he insisted that the head of security be in his office at the Clinic by 8:30 AM on Monday morning, followed by Dr. Ashe in his office promptly at 8:45 AM, with a full press conference arranged at 9:30 AM.

Given his plans were out working so well, and he was so damn happy lately, it was becoming difficult to act like an acrimonious, aloof egotist to his house staff and the staff at the Clinic. He also noticed that his good cheer was hampering his legendary temper and penchant for perfection at any hour of the day and night, but he knew full well that these eccentricities would be the required behavior to successfully culminate his plans. So, he would have to stick it out. Thank goodness for years of routine to help him through moments like this. Waking his entire staff up one hour earlier at 5 AM that morning, he wanted the pool ready for a long exercise swim followed by a massage, shower and shave, along with a breakfast of eggs benedict, fruit, and hot tea served on the veranda.

With things in motion and the press conference scheduled, the drive to the Clinic proved to be uneventful; no one was camped outside his home on the country roads, and no one tried to follow his chauffeured car into work that morning. As his limo approached the main gates of the Foundation grounds though, he saw the anchorwomen, newspapermen, and TV news vans littered outside. Everyone was nervously clamoring around, and he imagined that they were stressed and quite angry that they were not allowed to enter the private grounds until 9:00 AM to set up. Laughing lightly, he could only imagine how enraged they would be when he keeps the press conference to five minutes, but he needed them in a highly agitated state to finish this part of his plan.

As he entered the office, you could have heard a pin drop. Heads were low, the entire staff looked incredibly busy, and no one dared stare in Dr. Junger's direction. They could sense that heads were going to roll today, and they did not want to get caught in the line of fire and become collateral damage. Before Dr. Junger could utter a single word, his secretary, Marjorie, informed him that the head of security was waiting for him in his office and that Dr. Ashe would be there shortly, as instructed. God, the woman was efficient; there was hardly a task assigned to her that she wasn't able to tackle. If she wasn't in the later stages of her life, he would have recommended her to the Foundation for further education. She would have been an excellent administrator, whose work output alone would have allowed him to fire two or three of his less productive staff members.

After meeting with security, Marjorie brought him a cup of tea and the items that he had requested her to purchase for his meeting with Dr. Ashe, who timidly knocked at the door promptly at 8:45 AM. At five feet, seven inches with a balding head and rounded mid-section, Dr. Ashe was completely unassuming.

In contrast, Dr. Junger was a svelte, muscular, handsome, six feet three inches tall with a full head of perfectly maintained hair, grayed just enough for a sophisticated, intellectual, yet physically imposing presence. Dr. Junger motioned for Dr. Ashe to sit down at the round table next to his desk, which seemed like a positive sign. Dr. Ashe had not slept a wink all weekend when he got the call from Marjorie on Saturday morning that Dr. Junger wanted to meet with him. The fact that Dr. Junger had also called a press conference seemed like the kiss of death for his chances to keep his job. Firings always happened at a distance; so proximity was important for this meeting. Dr. Ashe had also noticed the Dunkin' Donut bag and cup of coffee at the round table. Perhaps there was some hope this morning. This was a personal touch that Dr. Junger had used only once before, when he promoted Dr. Ashe to assistant Clinical Director three years ago, but that was before the two incidents had occurred.

"Please, Dr. Ashe, make yourself comfortable and have some coffee and doughnuts. I assume that Boston Creme is still one of your favorites."

As Dr. Ashe sat down, Dr. Junger got up from his chair and walked to the window, which was several feet away; proximity was working in the opposite direction now. Dr. Ashe's forehead began to perspire, yet he noticed how well tailored the olive Armani suit was that Dr. Junger had on, and how beautifully the sun reflected in through the window, bringing contrasting, yet balanced areas of light and shade to the office. It was funny what your mind fixated on during stressful times. He remembered a class discussion on this at his university. There were interviews of people who had experienced life threatening accidents and survived. While they couldn't remember what had happened during the accident, they could remember the smell of the air, the color of the sky; it was as if their subconscious knew this could be the last moments of their life; so, it savored each second.

"Dr. Ashe, you have been with this institution for seven years; you were hired for your scholastic talent, impeccable work at previous institutions, and recommendations received from people that I respect. Now, everyone experiences a few bumps in the road along the way, and I would like you to know that the staff here at the Clinic believes that you have a good career in front of you. At times like these, it is important to leave the past behind you and looked straight ahead at the future; do you understand what I am saying?"

With half a mouthful of doughnut, raised eyebrows, and hopeful eyes, Dr. Ashe asked, "You mean you aren't firing me?"

"Why no, I am not firing you unless you refuse to sign this letter of resignation. After that, I am going to make it my personal mission to see to it that you never work in this field again. Your insipid behavior the last few years has cost this institution its valued reputation and its brand name. With all the intelligence that you have, it is amazing how incompetent you have become. I supported you once, but I will not go before the Board of Directors again and plead your case."

Nearly speechless, all Dr. Ashe could say was, "But you bought me doughnuts."

"Yes, Dr. Ashe," raising his voice so everyone outside could hear, "I bought you doughnuts because you seem to value them so much, which is my way of suggesting this as your new line of work. Perhaps you could work in a doughnut shop, eat doughnuts every day, counsel customers on the value of doughnuts, but never again step foot in this institution or try to work in this field again! Do I make myself clear! Now clean up your personal effects; you have thirty minutes left to leave."

"But thirty minutes, I..."

"If you are not out of here in thirty minutes, then I will have you personally escorted out of this facility—ah, Mr. Chambers, perfect timing. Dr. Ashe is leaving us in a half an hour; please see to it that he is on time."

Dr. Ashe whirled around and saw the head of security outside Dr. Junger's office.

"Now be a good boy, and sign this. We are also throwing in three months' severance pay to get you back on your feet, and maybe we'll even send you a Christmas card."

Dr. Ashe slid the paper into view, glancing at the sparse words reflecting his desire to pursue other interests. While he knew this was coming, he had hoped that he would be given another chance, but that was not his fate today. Signing the resignation letter, he picked up his doughnut bag and coffee leaving Dr. Junger's office with his head down.

Mr. Chambers stayed at the door. "Dr. Junger, I need to ask you one question. Everything is prepared for the press conference, as you had requested, but I am a bit confused on one set of instructions: I received an order to have Dr. Ashe's car towed off the grounds by 9:15 AM today. While everything is arranged, I have not given the go ahead for this yet. I wanted to double-check with you first, and, in light of what I overheard, why not let him just pack up and leave?"

"Mr. Chambers, please come in, close the door and sit down. I am glad that you checked with me, but I can assure you that this is how I want the situation handled."

"But why? Isn't he already embarrassed and humiliated enough?"

"Your security firm is on contract with us for another two years as I recall. Now, I don't question the decisions that you have to make in doing your job, and I would expect the same professional courtesy from you. So as long as we don't have an issue here, then I can assure you that I will vote for contract renewal with your security company when it hits the Board of Director's agenda." Pausing for effect, Dr. Junger waited for a response.

Matthew Chambers stared at the doctor; this was the side

of rich, powerful people that disgusted him. For some reason, they got off kicking weaker people around just so everyone knew who held all the cards. It was sickening, but he saw this behavior more than he would like to acknowledge from so-called well educated people.

"Alright, I got the message. I will comply with your request."

"Good, now please ask Marjorie to call a cab and have it at the front of this building by 9:30 AM sharp; she will know who to call."

Dr. Junger sat in his swivel chair, picked up his cup of tea, and turned toward the sunlight streaming in through his window as the Head of Security left his office. He had to admit that he was good; this present role fit him like a glove. He actually caught himself reminiscing for several minutes about the last forty-five years of this life. Was he really having second thoughts about what he would do in his next stage of life? Well, this always seemed to happen when his well-engineered plans were executed to perfection.

Marjorie interrupted his thoughts when she reminded him that the press conference would start shortly. Handing him a list of who was present, he noted that his adversary from the Inquirer was here, and that Bethany Caldwell from Channel 5 was also in the audience. Courting her for several months after his third divorce, he remembered how intellectual she was, which turned him on, but her culinary interests and bedroom skills were banal. They stopped dating after a while and became friends. Out of respect, he would answer her question first. Going over his succinct speech and anticipating exactly what would happen at the press conference in his mind since Saturday, he just needed to know who the players were in the audience to make last minute adjustments.

The press conference was set up at the exact spot where John Parella, Jr. jumped off the wall; this ironic gesture actually should help the press think of the first question that they should ask. While he never underestimated his adversaries, he did like to play with them a bit. As the press and TV station personnel watched Dr. Junger walk across the manicured lawns of this estate, several of them noted that he looked like an English lord walking from his manor to inspect the grounds and spend a few minutes with the common folk. His adversary from the Inquirer still thought he would always be an arrogant asshole.

Dr. Junger approached the podium and requested that everyone sit down. He merely stared at those who were still talking and fumbling around until it become apparent to everyone that he was not going to speak until everyone was seated and quiet. Looking at the wall, then at the people seated in front of him, he began.

"Thank you for coming today; it is unfortunate that the circumstances of this meeting are not dedicated to covering a more auspicious subject. Nonetheless, I am here to personally assure you today that the two egregious events that surrounded patients at the Clinic who have attempted suicide while in our care have been dealt with. In addition, I can assure you that security measures at this facility have been reviewed and corrective action has been implemented to ensure patient safety at all times. Now, are there any questions?"

The entire journalistic and broadcast community was stunned. They had to scramble over the weekend to line up coverage and crews for today. They had to arrive promptly by 6:45 AM and then wait for nearly two hours for their credentials to be checked, before setting up. Anyone who did not register at the first guard station by 7:00 AM was turned away, and, now that they were here, the press conference was nearly over. In unison the audience stood up and demanded to have their questions answered first.

"Ladies and gentlemen, please settle down so that your questions can be answered. I will take the first question from Channel 5; Bethany, go ahead."

"Dr. Junger, as we stand by the wall where John Parella, Jr.

attempted suicide, are you saying that proper measures had not been taken previously, and now such measures are in place to ensure patient safety?"

"Miss Caldwell, let me correct your summary just a bit. I am saying that the security measures at this facility have been reviewed and found to be followed to the letter. The security team hired for this facility is a nationally recognized firm, and this institution has the utmost confidence in their practices. The procedural issue found during our investigation was an administrative issue. The head doctor in charge must act in concert with the security team to ensure patient safety."

Channel 10 piped in without an acknowledgement from Dr. Junger. "Dr. Junger, isn't it rather convenient that both these instances happened when you were away?"

Dr. Junger replied, "Convenient, no; sad, yes. Another question, please." He looked straight at Peter Wilcock from the Philadelphia Inquirer.

"So, Dr. Junger, you claim no responsibility for two patients attempting suicide at your world renowned Clinic?"

"Actually, Peter, I take full responsibility. I take great pride in selecting the best doctors from around the United States to become members of our staff. I also take great pride in developing and mentoring my staff toward cutting edge patient care and administrative excellence. As you know, doctors who have worked here over the last thirty years have taken up key positions at institutions around the world. This is why I am so sad today. One of the people that I handpicked and was grooming as an eventual replacement to me here at the Clinic has acknowledged that patient care for the two individuals in question could have been handled better. As such, he has resigned, even though this institution still believes in him. One more question, please, then I have to go."

"What?" yelled Peter Wilcock. "You haven't explained hardly anything yet; who is the doctor that resigned today?"

Dr. Junger turned and pointed to the cab at the curb of the

clinical building. "I am sad to say that Dr. Ashe has resigned today. Thank you for your time. You may speak with Dr. Ashe if you wish, but my limo is waiting. I have other matters to address now." Security briskly escorted Dr. Junger to his vehicle by the main gate.

Again, the press and TV station personnel were completely stunned. What had just happened? None of them had a story, and they all looked at one another as if in a collective state of shock. One local press reporter had his head clear a few seconds faster than the rest, and he was running across the grounds to the cab where Dr. Ashe was still loading his personal effects. Then a mass frenzy hit, and like a school of piranha that had just been woken up by splashing water, they hungrily advanced across the lawn. Their prey was in sight. Dr. Junger had given them nothing, but Dr. Ashe would not get away until they had a story.

Before entering his limo, Dr. Junger turned just in time to see the whole crowd moving toward Dr. Ashe. The distance was a good quarter mile. It was a track meet out of control with stumbling, pushing, jostling for position, lane violations, and frequent cursing. It was comical to see his chain smoking adversary from the Philadelphia Inquirer in last place, hunched over, out of breath and still a hundred yards away from Dr. Ashe.

Meanwhile, the rest of the piranha had circled the man and were starting to bite.

Chapter 11

DR. DUHRING AT HOME

That Monday evening, Dr. Duhring was mentally exhausted when she arrived at her elegant home nestled away in Bucks County. Even at this hour of night, with little traffic, it was still a forty-five minute drive from the Grant Institute near Media to her home. Turning into the driveway at 8:35 PM with her windows open, she was pleasantly greeted by blossoming dogwoods, tall fully leafed oak trees, and the smell of fresh cut grass. With the sunset enveloping her home as she pulled into the small cul-de-sac in front of her house, she reminded herself how she fell in love with this twelve acre property five years ago. The home was built in the 1920s, and it still had the original two inch thick oak front door with a brass mail slot. While the stained wooden beams and plaster on the exterior walls of this two story Tudor home had been refurbished many times over the years, each restoration stayed true to the original character of the house. Although she paid a small fortune to add a back porch, a new cedar shake roof, and to update all the plumbing and heating throughout the home, it was nights like this that reaffirmed her previous decision, and she knew just how she would spend the rest of the night. After freshening up, she would eat dinner on the back porch treating herself to her favorite salad, consisting of walnuts and mixed greens blended with raspberry vinaigrette, served with a nice portion of warm brie, French bread, and several glasses of Pomerol, her favorite Bordeaux.

Setting her second glass of wine down, she observed the richness of the night. Darkness had fallen like a curtain across the sky; only the stars and fireflies provided any light at all. When she closed her eyes and listened, she could hear the deer stirring in the fields, and the distant bellow of bullfrogs from the pond toward the backend of her property. On nights like this, breathing in the fresh air, she often covered herself with a light blanket and fell asleep on the porch. Tonight was different though; she felt lonely and longed to share the intimacy of nights like this with a partner. She wanted someone intelligent and strong but sensitive enough to understand her private thoughts and dreams. Six years ago, at twenty eight, she fell deeply in love with such a man. Although he was much older and had three previous marriages, his charm, intelligence, sensitivity, and ability to listen made him the perfect partner. She was even willing to forego having children to be with such a partner. After a year of almost total bliss, she wanted him in her life forever, and she was sure, even to this day, that he was also in love with her—the way that he kissed her, held her, earnestly paid attention whenever she talked, and the way that he smiled at her when she walked into a room, conveyed all this.

When she pledged her love to him and confidently asked him to marry her, she was crushed when he refused. At first she thought that he was being coy with her, but, after several days, it became apparent that he meant it. She assured him that the age difference did not matter to her, and that she did not need to have children–that their love was enough for her. But he still refused to marry her, and, when all logic failed, she let her German temper loose until he told her why.

She remembered the look that he gave her when he sadly

gazed into her eyes and told her that he could never marry her because of professional differences. There would be times in the future where she would vehemently disagree with his decisions or a course of action that he felt obligated to pursue. Such professional discourse would tear their relationship completely apart; so, he would rather end their relationship now while they still had strong feelings of love for one another than to have their relationship degrade over time. She was astounded that he wouldn't even try, that he thought so little of their love and her to think that they couldn't work through difficult moments, that he had labeled her as not being flexible enough to provide leeway in a field where he was considered a genius, and she was a talented newcomer. At the time, she felt used, like a groupie discarded by a bored band member; years later she began to see that he was being honest: the only man that she ever truly wanted her entire life had unknown depths to him, fueled by a brilliant yet, at times, diabolical nature. Although his past accomplishments had shown that such actions lead to unprecedented discoveries, she had an inkling that his recent actions were not as altruistic as his previous ones were.

The next morning, she got up refreshed and went for a three mile run. Her house was adjacent to a forest preserve that was lined with well-worn paths and animal trails that the passive or avid jogger could partake in. Man-made trails went all the way from one mile jaunts up to a seven mile perimeter run with all the trails extremely well marked. In the mood for a fast, heart pumping run, she chose the hilliest course in the preserve.

While winded and a bit pink in the face at the end, it felt great to blow the stale air out of the tank, enabling her to take on the challenges of the day, which would include another scintillating session with Mr. Parella. While she thought that they had made good progress in their first few sessions, they had become bogged down lately. He was becoming evasive, refusing to go into any details on his dreams or what pressures he could have possibly faced to cause him to attempt suicide at the Clinic. He would no longer talk about his poetry, and he seemed to be having a little too much fun joking around with Stephen and Evan. The one bright spot was that his dour, depressive behavior exhibited a week ago seemed to be in check at the moment.

Well, perhaps it was time for a little tough love. If he didn't open up today, she had half a mind to cancel her sessions with him for most of this week and well into next week while prescribing additional sessions of physical therapy, including the weekends. Smiling to herself, six to eight days of double physical therapy sessions would bring any uncooperative patient to their knees. By mid-next week, she predicted Mr. Parella would be a babbling brook.

While brewing the morning coffee, she turned on Channel 5; although she preferred watching movies on the 27-inch TV in her bedroom, the 12-inch mini TV in the kitchen alcove was sufficient for local news and weather forecasts. Glancing down at the Formica countertops, she made a mental note for the fiftieth time to call about granite replacements. While this item had been on her home list for two years now, she entertained very little, and had no family in the area; so, it never made the top ten 'to-do' items at home. However, she always indulged herself on just how good granite counter tops would look in her kitchen.

It was then that her attention was diverted to a familiar voice. Looking at the small screen, she saw the unmistakable form of Dr. Junger at the Clinic giving his press conference. Even in his late sixties, his impeccable clothes, taunt athletic shape, and good looks made him an Adonis. He conveyed incredible confidence even in the face of adversity. She swore that he must have been dipped in Teflon at birth; no issue ever tarnished his image. But she was beside herself with anger when he pointed his finger at Dr. Ashe, and the press conference became a mad scramble to persecute him.

There on the television was her old friend Timothy Ashe,

clearly hurting and yet attempting to maintain a few ounces of dignity in his last minutes at the Clinic. Holding family pictures, pens, pencils, and a few other personal items in a cardboard box as the press surrounded him, no sooner would he stumble through one question when five other reporters would squeeze in, and trip him up with more. In summary, he admitted that he was in charge when both patients attempted suicide, that security protocol should have been handled better, that he was sorry for the embarrassment caused to Dr. Junger, the Clinic, and the Preston Family, that he had resigned, that he was saddened to leave the Clinic after seven years there, and that he just wanted to be left alone. The only question that he would not answer was if he was going to continue to work in this field again.

To make matters worse, the piece closed with Bethany Caldwell's synopsis of the situation, where she praised Dr. Junger and the Clinic for swiftly dealing with an unsettling situation, and then proceeded to paint Dr. Ashe as a once promising but clearly troubled young psychiatrist who must now reassess his life and future ambitions. Her piece ended with the camera panning on the cab as it and Dr. Ashe exited through the main gates. She all but hung a sign on Dr. Ashe that declared him damaged goods now and forever; no administrator would dare hire him after this. His career was over, which she expected is exactly what Dr. Junger had in mind, and he had gotten one of his ex-girlfriends to do most of the public dirty work for him.

Now that blame for the Clinic's problems had been publicly accepted by Dr. Ashe, she knew that Dr. Junger would want his patient returned to him under the guise of professional courtesy. But after what he did to Dr. Ashe today, it would be a hundred cold days in hell before she would allow that, yet she knew that she didn't have the clout to evade him indefinitely. Time was not on her side. In her career at the Clinic, Timothy Ashe had demonstrated his skills as a psychiatrist and an administrator to everyone including Dr. Junger; it was no fluke that he was promoted to Assistant Clinical Director, being handpicked by Dr. Junger for the post. Dr. Ashe's casual dress and affable nature created a phenomenal bedside manner. Patients were very comfortable with him. Given his reputation spread by word of mouth, people clamored for him to treat them. In his personal life, she had seen firsthand how loving he was to his wife, Clara, and their three children. So why would Dr. Junger let one of his star pupils become a public scapegoat? He had always stood firmly in his staff's corner on such matters before; his reputation alone could have easily handled this situation as he did so many times in the past.

She had to conclude that something bigger was at stake here; she couldn't see what it was, but she had to do her best to try and figure it out. Gritting her teeth in determination, she needed to reach Mr. Parella soon, for something had to link both suicide attempts at the Clinic. One patient attempting suicide is a fluke; two patients attempting suicide is a pattern. If they didn't want to kill themselves, and they were just calling out for help, then what was wrong with the psychiatric therapy at the Clinic? Why wasn't it working for these patients? Why couldn't the staff recognize and document these tendencies and take precautionary measures? Perhaps she had underestimated the situation; maybe Mr. Parella is somehow a victim here in a way that she couldn't understand. Perhaps the issues that he is struggling with really weren't on the surface and within his grasp to discuss. Maybe Mr. Parella needed a little memory boost. It would take a very skilled practitioner to reach Mr. Parella in such a way, and she knew just the person skilled enough to attempt it. Hopefully, Dr. Amello wasn't booked this morning.

Calling her secretary, she asked her to get ahold of Dr. Amello's administrative assistant and work something out—especially if Dr. Amello was booked this morning. Dr. Duhring had recognized a long time ago that secretaries held the true power in the office; piss them off, and it would take a month of Sundays to get an appointment with anyone, even if it was a top priority at the Institute. Treat them with respect and stay on their good side and scheduling nightmares were magically resolved.

Before seeing the news on Channel 5, Dr. Duhring was going to enjoy a leisurely pace for the morning having previously canceled John's session for today. Now, she had to hurry; the gloves were off, and the battle had already begun. She would have to formulate a phenomenal plan to take on Dr. Junger, but he was such a logical thinker and an astute mathematician, with an uncanny ability to predict outcomes and the probability of a person's actions once he got to know them. Unfortunately, Dr. Junger knew her quite well. But she also knew him, and, like most successful men, he had an ego the size of Manhattan, and on top of that he was an incurable romantic that loved red wine.

The rough outline of a plan was starting to take shape.

Chapter 12

BACK AT THE OFFICE

Dr. Duhring arrived at the office around 10:30 AM; traffic was always worse than expected especially when you needed to be someplace on time. Today was no exception as she scampered down the hall and took the stairs up to her office instead of the elevator. She was rounding the corner to her office while trying to catch her breath when she heard Ellen, her administrative assistant, assuring Dr. Amello that she would be there any minute. This was one more reason why she was going to have to break down and buy a cell phone like most other professional people. Her moral objections to owning a cell phone as being an electronic leash seemed like a moot point now, especially when she was late for her own meeting. The convenience and network breadth of cellular communication far outweighed her previous reservations, and who knows—perhaps they'll create digital assistants in the future that can analyze your tendencies and organize all your key activities. Now that would be useful.

Dr. Duhring composed herself and surged into the outer office. She said good morning to Ellen and Dr. Amello while grasping the latter by the arm and leading him into her office before anyone could utter a word. As she closed her door, seeing a relieved look on Ellen's face, she mouthed the words, "Thank You."

From the two Styrofoam cups of coffee and Danish crumbs on the floor in the waiting area outside her office, Ellen had done everything but tackle Dr. Amello to keep him there an extra fifteen minutes. Ellen was a gem, and she didn't know what she would do without her. Ellen always arrived at 7 AM and worked until 4:30 PM. Of the two of them, Ellen was definitely the morning person, who was tough enough to handle emergencies the minute she arrived at work, yet tactful enough to manage delicate administrative situations during Dr. Duhring's absence.

"Dr. Amello, I want to thank you for waiting for me; I must apologize for being late, but I have run into circumstances that require your expertise and professional advice."

"Well, I must say that I personally do not appreciate waiting for someone when an appointment has been so urgently requested, and I know that my patients, who were previously scheduled this morning, will also be unhappy with the short cancellation notice given to them. But, I am flattered that you would seek my advice, and I am curious how you managed to block out my entire morning for this, which means that this must be very important. So, how can I help?"

Dr. Duhring was so concerned with getting Dr. Amello to her office that morning that she didn't have the time to work out exactly what she was going to say to him. To make matters worse, she had read about his work, but knew little else about him. She was going to have to fumble her way through this without making it seem like she was wasting his morning.

Buying some time while wanting to bridge personal distance in the discussion, she asked Dr. Amello to move to the wicker chairs on the far left side of the room. Once they sat down, a fourteen inch diameter table was all that separated them. When Dr. Duhring was about to speak, she paused before doing so to compose her thoughts; out of the corner of her eye, she saw Dr. Amello's face take on a look of concern. He spoke first.

"Goodness, maybe this is more serious than I thought. What is going on?"

"Well, as you probably know, the Institute received a patient from the Clinic. This patient happens to be the second suicide attempt that they had there. At first blush, I thought nothing of it. From what I read of this patient previously and saw during the initial sessions, he seemed like another egocentric type-A personality that managed to screw up his marriage, his relationships with his family and best friends, and was now wallowing in self-pity and subsequent depression. I was quite confident that therapy would uncover that his suicide attempt was a belligerent, selfish act to get more attention and have other people, who once cared about him, feel sorry for him."

"So, do I assume that is not what you found?"

"Actually Dr. Amello, I found an intricate situation. Mr. Parella had solid parental role models; he came from a family that expected him to work hard, and he adopted a solid work ethic in order to be successful. Then, as things unraveled in his life, he knew enough to seek professional help, but that help has apparently fallen short of the mark. The documented sessions at the Clinic over the last six months reveal nothing of his present condition or the blocked areas that I have uncovered in my sessions with him. While I have to take into account that I only had him for a short period of time, my professional opinion is that I could try for months without unveiling these blocked areas and root-cause the issue or issues associated with his suicide attempt."

"Dr. Duhring, with all due respect, your involvement in this situation is only to provide an assessment of his mental condition and his future propensity for suicide as state law requires. I am sure that at some point in time the Clinic will want this patient back, especially now that the situation seems to have found a willing candidate, in Dr. Ashe at the Clinic, to take the blame for these suicide attempts."

"I knew Timothy Ashe personally, and while he may be somewhat complicit in not handling security matters perfectly, I can assure you that he is not the cause of these patients committing suicide, even though he was the attending psychiatrist in both cases."

"Ah, are you sure that this matter hasn't become personal? Didn't you work at the Clinic—didn't you have a relationship with Dr. Junger? Are you sure that you are not trying to find something here that is not there?"

Almost getting mad, she checked this emotion very quickly as Dr. Amello was a pragmatic doctor in his mid-fifties, who was well respected at the Institute; he was only pointing out the obvious to see how she would react. She viewed the next few minutes as crucial to winning him over.

Staring straight ahead and talking very softly, she knew that absolute honesty with someone she hardly knew was the only path that she could follow here.

"I have to admit that, when Mr. Parella arrived, I did relish the thought of receiving a phone call from Dr. Junger in order to have him state his case on why his patient should be returned to him. I planned on having him grovel through several phone calls before releasing Mr. Parella back to the Clinic. Shakespeare probably had it right about the wrath of a scorned woman. But I think a more fundamental issue is at stake here: this patient's overall care, initially with Dr. Junger and now with Dr. Ashe, seems to be off the mark. Professionally, I couldn't live with myself if I allow the matter to just go away. However, I am not ignorant in political matters; I am sure that Dr. Junger will exert considerable pressure to get his star patient back quickly if he wants him, and unfortunately, I don't have the tenure at this Institute to muster the kind of support to hold him off."

"Dr. Duhring, no one has the kind of backing needed to take on Dr. Junger. So in summary, you believe your time with Mr.

Parella is short, and you want my help to find a needle in a haystack, so to speak?"

Turning and looking straight at Dr. Amello, all that she could say was, "Yes."

"Can you tell me what we are talking about here? Are you asking me to perform some cursory hypnotic techniques, or are you asking for something more?" Dr. Amello slide to the edge of his wicker chair, awaiting the answer.

With a deep intake of air followed by a heavy sigh, Dr. Duhring answered, "Yes, I am asking you to do that, but if that doesn't work, then I am afraid that we may have to induce chemical hypnoses."

"That is absolutely out of the question; nothing in the few days of case notes that you could have collected would warrant such a course of action. Protocol at this facility strictly forbids such a move without written, signed authorization. Is there something that you haven't told me?"

In a low voice, Dr. Duhring reminded Dr. Amello that in an emergency situation she had the authority to initiate such a procedure.

Pointing his finger at Dr. Duhring, Dr. Amello's voice rose slightly. "Are you willing to risk your reputation and career, as well as mine, on a hunch, an intuition? For goodness sake, you are the Director of Psychiatry at this Institution—not a witch doctor!"

"I would take full responsibility." Doctor Duhring's voice was still low.

"I am not a child. I would be equally responsible for any adverse effects or outcome as you would be. Dr. Junger would drag us in front of the review board and have us tarred and feathered and run out of town forever, and then there are potential civil litigation concerns here also."

"Alright, how about trying some basic techniques, judging the responses, and then evaluating what next steps should be taken," Doctor Duhring suggested, looking at the man across from her straight in the eye.

"Sounds a lot like the approach to the Vietnam war to me — remember how that turned out?"

"Will you at least try? If you become uncomfortable at any time, then we can stop."

"I'll think it over, Doctor. I will let you know next week, but I am sure that my answer will be no."

"Could I get you to think it over in ten minutes and let me know? I want to get started at 11 AM today."

The request was so ridiculous that Dr. Amello could only stand there and stare at her. Seconds later, he spoke. "You're serious aren't you?"

She nodded her head without looking away from his gaze.

"Alright, I'll tell you what. I am going to go for a little walk, visit the men's room after drinking two large cups of coffee this morning while waiting for you in your office. If I come back to your office, then the answer is yes; otherwise, the answer is no." Mumbling to himself, he shook his head as he left her office.

At 10:59 AM, Mr. Parella, along with his orderlies, arrived at her office a bit confused. Yesterday, he was told that today's session was cancelled. Then an hour ago, he was told that it was re-scheduled for 11 AM. As John walked into the office, he noticed that Dr. Duhring had her hair pulled back in a bun, giving her a gentler look that seemed approachable by mere mortal men. Observing him looking at her, she caught herself critiquing her appearance. While she liked the white shirt, cotton pants suite and blazer that she was wearing, she hated to come to work with her hair in a bun. It was a casual look reserved for the weekends.

She decided to break the ice this morning with light conversation. "So, Mr. Parella, how is physical therapy going?"

"You mean physical torture, don't you?" responded John. The orderlies smirked.

"He's like a beached whale," Evan joked. "You keep pushing him out to sea, and he keeps returning to shore flapping his fins helplessly."

"Hey, I am not that bad! I can swim fourteen whole laps

before stopping now, lift some weights, stretch out like a rubber band, and I lost four pounds already."

Stephen joined in the fun. "You would have lost like fifteen pounds by now if you'd stop sneaking those breakfast rolls every morning after Dr. Duhring's sessions."

It was 11:02 AM, and although Dr. Duhring was enjoying the banter, her stomach was developing a queasy feeling.

"Well, it's Dr. Duhring's fault; she presses me to the point of mental exhaustion each day. I have to compensate for the mental calories burned up."

Deciding to enter the fray, she suggested that if her session was too stressful, then perhaps she should cancel her sessions and just prescribe double physical therapy sessions every day for the next month. That, coupled with eliminating the in-between meal breakfast rolls, should help Mr. Parella lose the excess weight, at which point he may even be somewhat physically attractive to some of the more questionable females in the facility.

Stephen and Evan were nearly rolling off the wicker chairs with laughter. It was now 11:03 AM and Dr. Duhring was nearing panic, but her outside demeanor was calm. Raising her eyebrows and tilting her head back while looking straight at John, she saw he had been caught off-guard. His eyes were glowing; his mind was spinning, trying to think of a response, but his mouth was still wide open ready to catch ten flies at once.

"Doc, that was brutal. Do you treat all your patients this way?"

"Only the pampered, self-centered ones," she replied.

Again, his mouth fell wide open, but this time she knew why. He had called her 'Doc,' and she did not correct him. She wanted to see how he handled this new level of familiarity.

11:04 AM, and still no Doctor Amello.

John held his hand to his heart like he going to say the pledge of allegiance. Instead, he sincerely stated how his mission in life was to change the doctor's opinion of himself with actions instead of mere words.

She wasn't going to let that go. "Gentlemen, let's all raise our feet; Mr. Parella has just informed us that he going to be spreading manure around this office for quite a while today."

John had to laugh now. Man, she was brutal, and he liked it. A feisty, good looking woman was definitely a turn-on. His smile faded though; she would never get involved with an overweight basket case like him, especially one who couldn't keep up with her intellectually and lacked confidence. For goodness sake, he didn't even like himself.

Dr. Duhring noticed John's change of mood; in the last few seconds, he became sad, but the reason for the sudden change was not apparent. Well, it was 11:06 AM, and she was quite distressed over Dr. Amello's decision; all that she could think of, at the moment, was to arrange a sequence of random questions to see if that would evoke a different response from John.

"Mr. Parella, what did you think of Dr. Ashe?"

"Whoa, that's different. I guess we're starting the session now. What exactly do you mean, Doctor?"

"What did you think of him as a professional?"

"Well, he was aces in my book, very personable. He seemed to genuinely care about me and his other patients."

"How do you feel about your brother?"

"My brother? Well, I love him, but I drove him nuts like all younger brothers do."

"What did you hope to achieve when you checked yourself into the Clinic?"

John was becoming more puzzled by the questions. Frowning, he answered, "Well I wanted help; I had hit an all-time low in my life, like we discussed before."

"Did you consider yourself suicidal when you entered the Clinic?"

John thought this over for a few seconds. "No, I don't think so. I mean, I was feeling pretty sorry for myself, but I didn't go there thinking that I would try to kill myself."

"What was the most romantic moment in your life?"

John frowned again. "Where is this going—romantic; what do you mean?"

"Mr. Parella, we are free flowing here—a stream of consciousness thing. Please hang in there with me. Now, what was the most romantic moment in your life? Not sex, romance."

"Okay, well, I would have to say it was my very first kiss."

"And when did this happen?"

"Well, I was thirteen; it was the summertime, and I met a girl at my cousin's summer party in Darby, Pennsylvania. We just looked at one another; we were attracted to each other, you know. We talked and walked around, and then we kissed. It wasn't just a peck either; it was a kiss that lasted for several seconds."

"And why do you remember it to this day?"

"Because it was my first kiss; it felt innocent and uncomplicated by all the other stuff in life."

"So, it was a kiss without commitment."

"Doctor Duhring, I was only thirteen at the time," John responded, a little frustrated.

"Did you ever see her again?"

"No, I never did. She was an Italian Girl; remember, their kisses are fatal. We've covered this ground before."

"When you sold your business to the venture capital group, did you ask the advice of your colleagues before the sale?"

"Yes, I did, but it was my company; I had devoted everything to it, and if I wanted to sell it, then so be it."

"Before when we talked, you said that you screwed your colleagues out of millions; so you really didn't care about the effect that it had on them and your relationship?"

"Hey, look, that's not what I meant. I listened to their advice, but I just felt that it was in everyone's best interest for me to sell the business and try to spend time with my family."

"From the sessions that you had at the Clinic, it was noted that your colleagues encouraged you, even begged you to take longer vacations with your family and spend more time during the week with them; they cared about you. Didn't you trust them to maintain the business while you tried to get the rest of your life in order?"

"By that point in time, I just wanted out; so, I decided to sell. It was my prerogative; I owned the majority interest in the company."

"Yes, you got your payday, Mr. Parella. Did you think that your colleagues deserved to get the boot when the venture capital group took over?"

Looking at the floor, John answered in a low voice. "No, they didn't deserve that."

"Do you think that Dr. Ashe should be held accountable for your actions at the Clinic?"

"It wasn't my fault that he got fired."

"Actually he resigned; so whose fault is it then?"

"Look, I went to the Clinic to get help. They are the professionals, and they are supposed to be able to detect stuff like this. That's what their paid for."

"So, Mr. Parella, you became suicidal while at the Clinic. Dr. Ashe was your primary psychiatrist; so, he should have known what you were thinking, whether you said anything or not."

"Well, yeah, I guess so; he is trained for this stuff, right? I was feeling pressured. The dreams and the things from those dreams played over and over in my head all day long. They were intense; they were steering me, and I needed to do something."

"Mr. Parella, how did you expect the Clinic, or anyone for that matter, to help you if you never opened up and talked about any of this?" Dr. Duhring was purposely showing frustration in an attempt to find a way into his private thoughts. John didn't answer; so she tried another angle.

"Are any of your dreams captured in your poetry?"

"Yeah somewhat, I wrote a poem about death."

"Is this also a sad poem?"

"Yes and no; its about a person who has become so weary and tired that he is no longer afraid to die and start a new life."

"The poem seems a bit morose. Is it somehow an admission that you had finally given up and wanted to commit suicide?"

"Jesus, no; it's a poem," John was becoming exasperated with the session, and he was close to shutting down.

"Okay, then are there things, as you put it, inside your head commanding you to act a certain way, or is it less complicated than that?"

"You're the ones that are supposed to figure that out," John barked in a stern voice. With this sudden change in tone, Stephen and Evan inched to the edge of the wicker chairs.

"Yes, we are Mr. Parella, but it is again obvious that you are not sharing key information to let us help you. Dr. Ashe was an accomplished psychiatrist before he ran into you; if you had shared information with him in the last six months, then I am sure that he would have been able to help you. Just as I am sure that we can help you here if you are willing to share information with us."

John looked back down at the floor and stared at it for several seconds without responding.

Damn, thought Dr. Duhring. She had pushed him too hard, and he was about to clam up for good. She would attempt one more tactic with him.

"So, what is it going to be? Do you want our help, or should I just schedule additional physical therapy sessions until the Clinic comes and claims you?"

John was puzzled; he looked up. "I thought that you were required by the State to complete a full psychiatric evaluation of me."

"Yes, an evaluation is required, but it doesn't necessarily have to be done by this institution. I could easily remand you back over to the Clinic and state it is in your best interest to do so. The Clinic has a secure wing that can handle such patients."

"I don't want to go back to the Clinic," John meekly replied.

"Why not, Mr. Parella?"

"They weren't helping me."

"You didn't let them help you."

"I suppose that is true, but..."

"But what? Are you willing to let people help you now? Are you willing to open up and trust that we want to help you?"

"You are going to think I'm absolutely nuts if I tell you about the dreams and the other things. I'll be in an institution my entire life! Hell, I think I'm nuts half the time, especially since I can't put all the pieces together and figure it out myself."

"We never refer to our patients as 'nuts'; they are people who need help, and if you let us help you, we will help you put the pieces together."

Looking straight at her, he answered angrily, "That's just semantics—when you people don't have textbook answers for things, then the patient is labeled a nut case, requiring endless evaluation. Why don't you all admit that sometimes you have no clue whatsoever as to what is troubling a patient? Why don't you all admit that sometimes you have no clue on how to reach a patient and help them? You even make jokes about patients! I hear what you all say when your off-duty, the jokes that you make. And don't tell me, Dr. Duhring, that you don't make any jokes about your patients."

This was an unexpected development. She was mulling this information over when she heard several soft taps on her closed office door.

"No, I won't lie to you Mr. Parella; privately, we do make some jokes about some of our more challenging patients. We are human after all, just like you. We have our faults too."

While John thought that over, she rose from her desk to see why Ellen was tapping on her door. When she opened the door, she saw Dr. Amello waiting outside. Elated, she went into the outer office and closed the door behind her.

"That was a long walk, Dr. Amello."

"Those were two very large cups of coffee."

"I see that you brought some equipment with you; let me brief you on the patient a little more before we proceed."

When the door opened again, John saw a new face enter the room.

"Mr. Parella, I would like to introduce you to Dr. Amello. I have asked for his assistance in helping you."

"Boy, you guys don't waste any time around here."

"I think Dr. Amello can help us unravel some of the areas that are, as you say, too complex for you to figure out. He is an expert in his field. Since it is getting a little crowded in here, Stephen, Evan, I would like you to wait in the outer office."

Evan spoke up. "Doctor, do you think that is a good idea? I'm a little concerned."

"Don't worry, Mr. Parella will be fine."

"But Doctor, hospital protocol requires our presence as a mandatory action in all sessions for at least the first month."

"It will be fine; I would like you both to wait in the outer office, alright? Do we have an issue here?"

"No, no issue Doc. We'll wait outside; c'mon Stephen."

Dr. Duhring frowned as they left her office. They had never questioned her before. She was curious about their reactions, perhaps even suspicious, but right now her plate was full; so, she turned her attention to John and Dr. Amello.

Chapter 13

AFTER BREAKFAST

"Mmmm, James, those pancakes were delicious, and I like eating them with fresh cut honeydew, strawberries and milk. Now if only we had some durian, then the meal would have been perfect," SuiLeng sighed.

PekBing and Chun Soon looked at one another and cringed. Neither of them liked durian either. James motioned to the boys and acted like he was putting his finger down his throat and gagging. Both boys covered their mouths and giggled.

SuiLeng just looked at all of them. "None of you have a cultured taste. If I left it up to the three of you, you would eat macaroni and cheese or grilled cheese sandwiches all week long. Now you two monsters get upstairs and pack; I am going to inspect your clothes selection in thirty minutes."

"Aw, Mom, we know how to pack," whined PB. He was the oldest of both boys, at seven years of age. CS was two years younger, and even more mischievous than his older brother.

"Yes, let's see the last trip we took. Between the two of you, you packed two pairs of socks, one nice shirt, no underwear, and no dress shoes. But you both had at least three pairs of flip flops and five bathing suits apiece along with all your other swim gear. I have great confidence in you both. Now get going before I give you both wedgies."

"Mom, you aren't allowed to give us wedgies! Moms don't do that," CS piped in, a concerned look on his face.

"Oh yeah? We'll see about that! First one I catch gets a grand wedgie." SuiLeng jumped off the barstool in the kitchen and chased both boys half way up the stairs. They screamed and hollered half out of fun and half because they thought she meant it.

James was cleaning up the dishes when she returned. "You know, you need to do more of that with the boys."

SuiLeng gave him the "oh, is that so" face with the additional flare of both hands on her hips. "You know, you're absolutely right; instead of cleaning the house, driving the boys to the park and to soccer practice, shopping for food and clothes for everyone, giving the boys a bath, ensuring that they do their lessons, cooking, and giving up any personal time for myself so that I can freshen up and look pretty for my husband when he returns home from work, I will just play with the boys."

James shook his head. "That's not what I said. I am just suggesting that somewhere in that ten thousand item list that you put together each day that you could schedule in some fun time with the boys."

"Okay, smart guy, look at my day planner and tell me what to take off each day, and then tell me who is going to do what I don't do."

"I give up; you win. I don't understand why you can't take a little constructive feedback without getting upset."

"Okay, tell you what. I will hire a full time maid, and you can cook dinner each night so that I have time to run some errands and play with the boys. How about that?"

"SuiLeng, that is fine with me. You know that we can afford it, and I like to cook. I only have one concern."

"And what is that?"

With a serious look on his face, James said, "I don't want any grandmas for maids; they need to be very attractive. Otherwise, you know, it's going to be difficult for me to be inspired for the evening meal."

"Come here, you," grabbing James' terrycloth robe with both her hands. "First of all, you can't even handle one woman, and second, do you know why Asian doctors are the best in the world at microsurgery?"

"No."

"Because Asian wives cut the peckers off their husbands when they find out that they have been fooling around, and Chinese women are the worst. Do you want to know why Chinese women are the worst?"

"Not really, but I think you're going to tell me anyway."

"Yes, James, I am going to tell you. Chinese women are the worst because they cut it off and throw it in the ocean for fish food. Now get upstairs and pack before I give you a wedgie."

"But I'm not wearing any underwear," James retorted.

"Would you like to find out how Chinese women give men wedgies when they are not wearing underwear?"

"No, I think I'll pass on that."

"You get smarter each and every day that I am with you."

While they packed, SuiLeng asked James about the calls with Father Martin and that other man, who she later found out was called Dr. Junger. SuiLeng wanted to know why Father Martin was so upset with him, and how James met Dr. Junger. He told her that both situations were related, but each was a very long story. What she needed to know right now was that Father Martin did not want them to ever leave Florida, and that Dr. Junger was forcing their hand to do just that. She also needed to know, that if they ever left Florida, they would be followed and would be in danger.

SuiLeng asked the obvious question. "If we are safer in Florida, then why not just stay here after our Disney vacation?"

James walked over to her and put his left hand on her cheek, then rubbed her bottom lip with his thumb. "If I thought that we would still be safe in Florida, then I would stay here forever with you and the boys. I don't think that is true anymore; we are on borrowed time now, but I promise you nothing will happen to you and the boys. This time around I will hunt first, and no one will harm the ones that I love ever again. However, we have to change our vacation plans immediately; we have to leave the States now."

"We'll get through this together; my family can also help us."

"SuiLeng, I am counting on your family helping us. That is why I want to get us all to Penang as fast as possible. You also need to know that your brother and I had a history together before I met you."

"My brother told me a lot about you before I left Asia after the first time that we met. Knowing all that I know, I still chose to marry you." She then wrapped both her arms around James and kissed him; a kiss of passion, a kiss of love, a kiss of trust that carried her world and her children's world and their fate together toward the future.

Chapter 14

THE DESERT AWAITS

Islamic Year: 1377 AH   *1958 AD*

John Parella, Sr. left the King's rail car in a daze. He thought about his wife, his boys, and what the King had requested. It would have been easy to just finish his term of employment and return home to continue building a better life for them, which is why he came to Saudi Arabia in the first place. They would be able to buy their own home outright and provide a good initial education for their children. But if he followed through on what the King asked, then the future of his family, as well as his reputation and perhaps even his life, would be in jeopardy.

Looking up at the stars and breathing in the heat coming up from the desert as it rose into the darkness around him, he reminded himself that, at moments like this just as he was taught in the Navy, a person had to step up above their personal desires and fears. Such a decision is always based on trust, and he trusted the King implicitly. He marveled at how the King was implementing his vision for Saudi Arabia, and how he dealt with the various factions, tribes, governments, and enemies within and around his country. And on top of this, the Royal family now carried an additional burden for the entire world.

How does one go about handling the master plan for this world and the universe without creating complete religious and political chaos? Putting things into perspective, he had a rather small part in a much bigger plan. For now, his role was to only draw attention; let the interested parties investigate what he was doing, and buy the Royal family time to do whatever they had to do in the next several months. And if he could do this without getting himself killed — that would also be a good thing.

John took the King's advice to heart; the best plan was to be completely open. He showed his ceremonial knife to everyone, including his buddies, the trainees, etc., while taking extra time to show it to the new mid-level government officials, who were taking a more hands-on-approach in oil operations as more power was transferred from the King. The rehearsed speech included words of gratitude that the King spoke when he gave him and Mr. Jiling each a ceremonial knife, and how proud he was to receive such a gift. If anyone wanted to know what he and the King talked about, he would drone on and on about the Date Gardens and Oasis at Hofuf, the prophet Mohammed, the Hajj as well as the decorations and pictures in the King's private train cars. After two weeks, no one was interested anymore in his conversation with the King.

At this point, John felt comfortable enough to carry out the rest of the King's request. Months ago, he submitted a plan to Mr. Jiling on training his replacement.

Jahleel was a natural born leader of men that had become an accomplished mechanic, earning respect from his men and the new trainees that he lead because, even with his higher status, he never talked down to them or lectured them. He always took the time to show the men how things worked and to relate disparate pieces of information together until the men understood the mechanical complexities involved in their maintenance roles. Jahleel's crews could tear down and re-install a diesel engine faster than any other crew, and they could detect crazing in wheels that lead to thermal breakdown as well as refurbish/balance a brake system better than any state-side mechanic. His three year maintenance record showed that locomotives and freight cars, which his teams serviced, had the lowest mean-time-to-failure rate that was almost an order of magnitude better than any other crew. Mr. Jiling had assumed that John would pick Jahleel for his replacement, but he wanted some assurances that Jahleel had gotten all the horse play out of his system. An incident a half year ago still gave Mr. Jiling some reason for concern.

"John, are you sure that it is a good idea to put Jahleel in this role? Do you remember what happened six months ago?"

"Mr. Jiling, I give you my word that Jahleel has learned his lesson; it will be important for the men to see that he has overcome any immature behavior and can act responsibly. He still has some coursework to complete on crane operation and maintenance, but he has mastered everything else. If we don't do this, it will indicate a lack of confidence on our part with Jahleel; he will lose status with the men, which won't bode well for continuity of operations when I leave."

"Alright John, I'll go along with this, but I am holding you personally responsible. You have an excellent track record in your time here, and I would hate to see anything mare your permanent record and force me to withdraw my offer as being a personal reference for you when you return to the States and seek new employment."

Jahleel's previous horseplay was centered on holding the record for the longest operation in the red zone for a crane's engine. Knowing every engine part intimately, it was as if Jahleel could feel an engine's ability to handle stress and know just when to back off. Such was the case until he began showing off even more for the new recruits and sent a piston through the outer engine casing. This was not the behavior that a master mechanic's crew should be emulating.

Jahleel's last test for certification would be three weeks from now. Although mechanics were primarily responsible for locomotive and equipment maintenance, they also had to be certified on crane operations in case there was a shortage of operators. All he had to do was slowly and safely use the crane to lift up six pallets of axle bodies, train wheels, and journals from the freight cars. In addition, he had to be his own boom man to demonstrate that he knew what a safe cable wrap looked like around equipment attached to a crane. A falling load would crush a man to death, and a poorly attached cable could cut a man in half if it came loose or broke during a lift.

John Parella, Sr. had always drilled into each person on the maintenance team that the first rule for all serviced equipment before it leaves the service area is to check and double-check that the oil level in the equipment was full but not overfilled. Giving Jahleel a gentle reminder of this the day before his test, he also promised that he would check the levels after Jahleel did.

Jahleel was halfway through his test when he felt the crane engine shudder; the instructors around him were yelling at him to stop as oil poured out of both oil cases. The screeching of all the pistons seizing in the engine block and welding themselves in place soon overcame all the noise around Jahleel. Further chaos ensued as the abrupt jolt from the engine seizing caused the heavy load to bounce up and down at odd angles, snapping the crane boom in half.

Mr. Jiling was already running out from his office with more smoke coming out of his ears than from the crane's engine; he was about to unleash all his anger toward Jahleel, when John stepped in front of him and caught most of the tirade head on. No one had ever seen Mr. Jiling so mad before. To make matters worse, John was dragged into Mr. Jiling's office to continue the conversation, which escalated into a screaming and shouting match. When John exited his office, the instructors thought that Jahleel had been sacked. Things cooled down a day before another screaming match erupted in Mr. Jiling's office, when John continued to recommend Jahleel as his successor. John had backed Mr. Jiling into a corner by refusing to nominate or work with any other candidate as a successor; therefore, Mr. Jiling had no choice but to allow Jahleel to continue on that path.

The following day, both Jahleel and John were in Mr. Jiling's office. It was a one way conversation; Mr. Jiling gave the men two weeks to dismantle, transport, and re-assemble a crane from Bahrain, or he would fire both of them. Today of all days, Mr. Jiling had just received strict orders from the Minister that, until further notice, all scrap metal was to be buried in the desert instead of trying to salvage and ship it. With the replacement crane engine and boom lead-time from Germany at twenty-eight weeks, Mr. Jiling had no option other than to call his boss and request a crane from Bahrain, which was a conversation that he was not looking forward to.

After they left Mr. Jiling's office, Jahleel spoke first. "Mr. Parella, I want to thank you for still believing in me and allowing me to finish my training."

"Jahleel, you deserve to be my replacement based on your work record and your work ethic. Everyone knows that, including Mr. Jiling; however, his confidence is shaken; it will take sometime to restore his trust. I also want you to know that I suspect this situation was not your fault, but we'll try and figure out what really happened later on, if we can. Right now we need to get moving to keep both our jobs."

"Yes, I understand. I already have two crews ready; one crew will go with us to Bahrain; the other crew will stay here and prepare the large bay for crane reassembly."

It took one day to get to Bahrain, plus one half day to wait and receive a blistering reprimand from Mr. Jiling's boss, at which point Jahleel learned that he would be on probation for the next six months. John learned that he would not receive any recommendation to work with the American Oil Company in the States, and that he would only receive the standard boilerplate letter of recommendation from Arabian American Oil Company for future employment opportunities. The point being made was that the time John spent in Arabia would do very little to help him secure future employment anywhere. In addition, John and Jahleel also learned that the two week time period given to get this crane on line was no joke; it was a strict condition of their continued employment. It was also noted that if anything happened to this crane, even a little paint chip, then they would no longer be employed.

Other than sharing a nervous laugh when Jahleel commented to John that management "seems truly pissed," the men said very little on their way back to Dammam. Because there were many cranes on-site in Bahrain, it was very easy to remove the boom, wheels, and axles from one of the larger cranes and secure it to several freight cars. Without another crane on the other end though, they faced a daunting task to get the new crane on line in the time given.

But Jahleel's ingenuity came through. The crew that had stayed in Dammam had welded steel I-beams together and created custom flat bed skids to allow the new crane body, boom and ancillary parts to be easily transported into the large assembly bay. They also had welded additional I-Beam supports on many hydraulic chain systems to safely lift and align the crane body to all other sub-assemblies. Even with all this in place, it took a week and a half of eighteen hour days to complete the task on schedule, but men readily volunteered to work extra shifts in order to finish the work on time.

John's decision to back Jahleel had clearly earned him the additional respect of every instructor, working man, and trainee in Dammam who had never worked with him before, and those that knew him admired him even more. But he could tell that he lost status with the new mid-level government officials on site after seeing the smiles on their face and hearing them laugh as they walked past him. They all thought he was a fool for backing Jahleel. Their initial appraisal of John would change even more in subsequent weeks.

The orders from the Minister were quite extensive, covering a large range of scrap material from the oil rigs as well as the train transportation system. Overall, three major dump sites had to be dug with each dump site having specific depth and width dimensions, depending on what was being buried. At each dump site, he was to also pour in several metric tons of sea salt, which came from the desalination plants along the ocean, in order to dissolve the scrap metal over time.

The work crews needed one month to install equal miles of the special tracks at the three different dump sites around Dammam, Abqaig, and Ghawar. However, it was the realization that the new crane could lift whole freight cars and locomotive sections that created the buzzing of new mid-level government officials. An endless line of questioning, along with the same repetitive answers from John, persisted throughout the entire project. It played over and over again at each site.

"Mr. Parella, why are the rail cars not being disassembled before being buried?"

"Because the new crane from Bahrain can easily handle the weight of these items without causing damage to it," John would answer.

"But Mr. Parella, how can I inspect each rail car to ensure that it does not contain any item that shouldn't be scrapped? If it was completely disassembled then I would be certain that everything was properly handled."

"Well, I could wait for you to inspect all the material for each dump site before any scrap is dumped into it."

"It is very interesting, Mr. Parella, that the new crane has this capability, and that the track material to use a much heavier crane was ordered well ahead of the old crane being damaged."

"Yes, it is fortunate."

"Why is this device being added to each dump site? What does it do?"

John held the device in his hand. "It's called a beacon. I don't know why it is being added, and I really don't know what it does, but I am required to put it in each dump site to close the job ticket."

"You're very accommodating, Mr. Parella, but you haven't told me anything, and you don't seem to know very much."

John answered, "I am just following the work orders; perhaps, you should ask the officials at the Ministry if they have more information for you."

"I am an official from the Ministry, Mr. Parella!"

Only once was the situation escalated in a special meeting called in Mr. Jiling's office. The new government officials insisted that all rail cars be dismantled, or the job would be shut down.

Nervous about this meeting, Mr. Jiling answered very cautiously. "Certainly, we trust your judgments in all matters. I am sure that this is a simple misunderstanding. I will immediately offer my apology in writing to the Minister, and I will state that the misunderstanding is on our end and that the situation is being rectified immediately. In addition, I will state the new work schedule and cost-adders for completing the remaining part of the project per the intended instructions."

"It is not necessary for you to write an apology to the Minister; we will tell him how you handled the situation when it was brought to your attention."

"I am most sorry," stated Mr. Jiling, "But company policy requires me to document all orders that were not handled correctly; in this instance, I would be required to document in writing why I did not handle the Minister's orders correctly. Company policy also requires me to apologize in writing for any non-compliance and to separately document where the process broke down in order not to have such an event happen again in the future. My hands are tied in this matter now that it has been brought to my attention."

The room was quiet for a few seconds. Then, the most senior member of the group replied, "Mr. Jiling, in the spirit of cooperation, no one wants to cause you any personal embarrassment over this matter. Perhaps it is best to just state among us that we all learned something from this matter. Please continue the salvage operation as you have been doing. In the future, we will come to you directly on such matters, especially since Mr. Parella has only a few months left anyway."

Seeing that everyone had made their point and still had their dignity intact, Mr. Jiling agreed with them. With that, all the government officials left, Mr. Jiling replied with the proper salutations, and then he asked John to remain in his office.

"John, you have no more friends left over here. I am not even going to ask why you let this situation get to this point. You could have told me about this weeks ago; at that point, I would've had time to smooth things over. Frankly, the fact that you are leaving is probably the only reason that this issue hasn't escalated further. Take some advice from me, my friend, you better fix whatever is troubling you before you get back to the States; otherwise, no one is going to hire you."

A deep sigh summed up all of John's thoughts; all he could say was "Are we done?"

"Yes, we are done John," replied Mr. Jiling, *"We are definitely done."*

Chapter 15

THE FLIGHTS

Having taken a very early flight, Father Martin arrived at the Philadelphia airport, late-morning, on a rainy Tuesday. According to his mother, April and May rainfall was still three inches below normal in the Northeast, and the reservoir was a foot and a half lower than normal after winter. Wondering if today's rainfall would help the situation, he got his answer when he had to pull off the road twice in his rented vehicle due to the intensity of the downpours. Most of his family lived in the Springfield area, and, although they were disappointed to hear that he could only visit them for a few hours while he was there, they had come to understand over the years that his work extended to many families across the world. God had given him the calling to help others, and they were proud of him for dedicating his life to this pursuit.

However, at fifty-four years of age, Father Martin was becoming weary of this work; his assignments over the last seventeen years were never mundane, but the mental and physical duress experienced during that time had taken their toll. As a reward for his service, he had been allowed to call Florida his home base, moving to Deerfield Beach five years ago, and settling down at Saint Ambrosia. Now, he only took on a few assignments a year while also being one of the priests on staff. Long term, he was hoping to stay there and retire. Though the Bishop was pleased enough with his work in the last decade to call out his place of retirement, the glowing reports on Father Martin would take on a different tone once the Bishop found out the real reason that he had taken a sudden leave of absence.

Although Father Martin had extensive latitude to follow his instincts on assignments, he never circumvented Church Hierarchy and protocol by taking on a case before fully briefing his superiors and then receiving the framework from which he was to operate in. While this process was agonizingly slow and even more so with complicated cases, the entire resources of the Church were at his disposal when using this process. This time, he was going solo, and he was nervous because he didn't have a plan.

Being driven by his belief that James wasn't an evil aberration, an anomaly of nature, he sensed that James' presence meant something, yet he wasn't smart enough to figure it all out. To make matters worse, James was about to change himself forever; a move that James felt would enable him to protect his new family. Father Martin might have been able to rationalize James' decision, and perhaps even explain James' decision to his superiors, if he didn't have the sneaking suspicion that James was acting exactly like his antagonists wanted him to. And if that was the case, then what knowledge did those people possess that enabled them to remain confident of controlling James as he evolved? These thoughts troubled Father Martin while he drove down I-95 South toward Elkton, Maryland.

———∞———

James and his family started their journey to Asia by taking a flight out of West Palm Beach to Atlanta. From there, they traveled to Portland, and then they took a flight to Tokyo, Japan. While James and SuiLeng could have talked at any time during the trip, each of them felt more comfortable engaging in serious conversation once they were out of the United States.

The Tokyo Airport was a bit of a pain; few signs were in English, and they had to take a bus to Terminal 1. SuiLeng was again reminded of James' unique talent as he easily conversed in Japanese to find their way to the Terminal 1 bus stop. Even the boys were amazed, asking James how many languages he spoke, to which he responded "a lot." They knew James well enough by now that when he gave short answers, it was best not to ask any more questions. It was times like this that made James mysterious, which was cool to the boys; sometimes, they wondered if he was really a secret agent, which would be super awesome.

SuiLeng had brought along several games for the boys to play in order to pass the time. When she pulled out a miniature chess board, they simultaneously pleaded for anything else. Knowing how to motivate them and still make things interesting, she told the boys to walk quickly around the terminal area that they were in four times without running; the winner would get $5 and the loser would get $2. In addition, if they played three games of chess, then she would let the winner of the chess games pick two fun activities on the trip, while the loser picked one.

Suspicious, PB tested for understanding. "You mean if I win, and I choose to go swimming on two days, then we have to do that. And if CS loses, he can still choose to go swimming with his choice?"

"You boys catch on quick."

With that both boys were tearing around the terminal in a fast walk. CS was disqualified for running, but he didn't mind; he still got $2. Buying food and drinks while James took the boys to the restroom, she settled the boys down half a row away from them so that she and James could talk privately. The one thing that SuiLeng liked about the Japanese people is that they respected a person's private space; no one endeavored to listen to their conversation as they passed by or to sit too close to them as it appeared, from their body language and gestures, that they were discussing sensitive matters.

SuiLeng wanted to know more about James' conversation with Father Martin and more about this Dr. Junger person; she hadn't heard that name before. While they snacked on small sandwiches and fruit, James told SuiLeng both stories.

"There are several connections between my past, Father Martin, and Dr. Junger. I may ramble a bit as I try to explain all this to you; just stop me and ask questions if it doesn't make sense. Let me start with how I really met Father Martin."

SuiLeng breathed out deeply and shook her head slightly. "I will give you one thing James; life with you is never going to be boring, is it?"

"No, I don't think so. I met Father Martin at a Church nearly four years ago. I was lost again; the purpose of my life was blurred. The first time that I became lost was after my first wife-to-be was murdered."

James noticed that SuiLeng smiled a little when he mentioned Sunflower. It felt good to be able to talk about her. James never thought that he would ever meet another woman that he would care so deeply about again, yet here was SuiLeng right in front of him. Reaching out, touching her hair, he continued.

"After I avenged her death, I became a killer, a vigilante. I would camp all along the Chesapeake and Delaware Bay during the spring, summer and fall. During the worst of winter months, I returned to the tribe that raised me, because I was always welcome there. When Indians attacked other Indians unjustly, I avenged their death; if a white man attacked or killed an Indian, their demise was quick. When the white men killed each other, I did nothing. At that time, I hated them all."

"How did you know if a killing was unjust? Were you able to talk to or communicate with all the victims like you did with Sunflower before her death?"

"Yes, for several of them I was able to do just that. But with most I had to depend on the animals to tell me what happened. Back then, I was pure, and they were willing to trust me."

SuiLeng's eyes widened; her jaw dropped. "Oh, c'mon James, are you telling me that you can talk to animals? Are you kidding me?"

"No, SuiLeng, I was born with that gift, and what was most amazing is that the animals understood the Indian way of life because it was balanced with nature. Nature allows for killing to live; the animals all understood this and accepted it. Fish eat the bugs on the lake, and the hawks eat the fish. Rabbits eat the grass, and foxes eat rabbits, and a bear eats any darn thing that it wants to. Indians would hunt all of them, but only take what was needed to live, just like the animals did."

"You are blowing me away! Which animals are the smartest? Could you trust them all, and what did you mean by pure?"

"Oh boy," James sighed, "We really got off on a tangent. Alright, let me briefly answer your questions so that we can get beyond the animal thing and back to Father Martin. The stupidest animals are mosquitoes, ants, butterflies, and bees; there isn't enough brain matter to have full conversations, and what is there is like a programmed tape that runs continuously for their entire life. Snakes and spiders I would never trust; they're intelligent, but they only care about themselves. Now foxes, wolves and bears were really cool; they have a social structure and hierarchical rules for their society, but they all had egos, especially the males."

"Oh, what a revelation, males in other species have egos. I never would have imagined that! You all must have had a lot to talk about, then."

"Shall I continue or do you have any more caustic remarks to make?" A slight wave of the hand from SuiLeng was his signal to continue.

"During these years communicating and communing with the animals kept me sane; it was a very sad day when they would not talk to me or trust me anymore."

Curious, SuiLeng asked, "What caused that?"

"When I became un-pure."

"What do you mean 'un-pure?' This is the second time that you said that; did they take offense to your killing for vengeance?"

"No, they understood why I killed—they took offense when I interacted with another woman."

"You mean you became un-pure by being with another woman, but you were intimate with your first wife-to-be, and that didn't break their trust in you? I don't understand."

Looking down, James continued in a low voice, "Well, I have thought about that a lot; I can only guess that the love between Sunflower and I must have been considered pure or balanced. The love and respect that we had for one another and all living things around us must have been apparent. They still trusted me, until I became intimate with a woman that I really did not love, then the animals stopped trusting me."

SuiLeng had that look in her eyes again. "Well I think that I agree with the animals—I wouldn't trust you either if you had relations with a woman that you didn't love. How often did that happen?"

"Look, we're getting a little off track here," James said, exasperated. "I mean my goodness; after living for several hundred years, don't you think that I might have been with a few women over that time?"

"Yes, James, I would expect that you would have been with several women over that time. I am just wondering what feelings you had for them—or did you just use them? So go on, I want to hear more about the woman that made you un-pure."

"Oh my, alright. I had camped near a stream in late spring. It was early in the morning, and the fog bank was still lingering in the forest. I heard a gunshot, then loud voices. Running just below the ridge line, I saw two white men, a tall white woman, and her little girl, who seemed to be gathering water for morning breakfast. As I broke through the clearing, the woman had her back to me, but the look of panic on the little girl's face instantly conveyed that they were in trouble; without hesitation, I charged across the stream. The man that held the woman threw her to the ground and got off a shot that went clean through me, just below my left clavicle. Staggering a half step from the impact, I threw my knife deep into his throat. The other man fired a shot that glanced off my head. Disoriented and in a daze for several seconds, he came at me plunging his knife into my ribs, breaking a few of them. I remember hearing them crunch, then he stabbed my right leg. After I fell to the ground, he jumped on me and attempted to put his knife right through my eye before I grabbed his wrist and broke it. I can still see the look of panic on his face when I smiled while breaking his wrist; he realized a little too late that I was not really human, and that my tolerance for pain was incredible. Two seconds later, I snapped his neck, with one hand, leaving both men for the animals to have."

"The white woman picked up the gun and pointed it at me. Confused by her reaction until I remembered that I looked like an Indian, I told her in perfect English, "No, stop, I am a friend."

"This startled her, but the little girl, who must have been around seven, came right over to help me; they carried me to their cabin and cared for me. The wound to my head was more serious than I thought, as bone fragments had actually pressed against my brain. I couldn't feel the left side of my body as they carried me to the cabin. It took several weeks for me to fully recover from all the wounds. They were both amazed that I lived at all."

"Although still groggy for days, I had picked up their native language, which was Swedish. Losing control of my ability to stay one color while I was healing, I kept turning red to white and back again the whole time that I was in bed. Although they didn't speak of it at the time, I saw them stare at one another for several seconds when it happened. On the twelfth night that I was there, the mother began washing my wounds, which she always did after her daughter fell asleep. Washing my chest and arms, she then gently pushed me sideways to clean my ribs, shoulder, and legs. Rolling me back over, removing my loin cloth and her clothes, she touched me with her hands and body in ways that were very erotic. I had never experienced lust before; it was a new set of emotions for me."

"I stayed with her and her little girl until early fall; the hunting, trapping and trading that I did for them earned enough money for them to go back home. Her husband had died from pneumonia the year before; so, she and her daughter were lonely and scared. They had no family to help them in this new world; helping them also stopped me from killing for the time being."

"However, when I tried talking to the animals again, they shunned me. When I asked why, they told me that my scent had changed, and had become un-trustworthy. They sensed that I was not hunting out of need anymore, that there seemed to be a new motivation in me, and because of this, I could no longer commune with them or connect to them as I had before. For weeks, I was stunned, but I knew they were right. Wanting to protect this woman and her daughter caused me to think differently about men, women, and families after that. The time that I spent with her and the little girl also made me yearn for a family of my own."

"Humph, so James, you both used each other, but it was an agreeable relationship wasn't it? They needed money to return home, and you got sex in return?"

"SuiLeng, there were some feelings there, but not like with Sunflower or you. I was very young at the time — how can you even be upset at all? That was almost three hundred years ago."

"James, women love more intensely than men do. I don't know why, but it is just the way that it is. So, yes, I am actually upset with this Swedish woman, and not for what she did, but because of the look on your face when you remembered being with her. It hurts me because you could not detach yourself from the emotions that you felt at the time when you re-told the story.

Even though I realize that she has been dead a long time, and I have nothing to fear from her; I am still going to get up, take a little walk around, and then go to the restroom. Hopefully, when I return, that stupid grin that men usually have when recalling their previous exploits will be gone from your face. But before I go, how many other promiscuous periods have you experienced in your lifetime?"

SuiLeng got the answer that she was hoping not to get when James couldn't even answer and had to look away from her gaze; she briskly walked away. James sauntered down to where the boys were playing chess. Before James could casually ask who was winning, PB asked James what he had done to get Mom so mad. After James told them that he was just talking, they told James that is how they get into so much trouble themselves.

PB had the best advice. "Well, all I can say is that mom likes the truth, but if the truth gets you in more trouble, then its best to be completely quiet and say nothing at all, or come up with such a whopper of a story that she starts laughing." After that advice, James knew that he was in a ton of trouble.

When SuiLeng returned, James tried to continue the previous conversation to which SuiLeng abruptly responded, "James that conversation is in the past; let's move on. I have said all that I have to say on the matter. Hopefully, you learned something from the conversation. And I don't want to see that indignant look that is on your face right now."

The look presently on James' face was a mixture of unspoken thoughts. One thought was that if he ever tried to end a conversation as she just did; she would go ballistic. The other thought etched on his face is one that men all over the world have at one time or another when they ponder why they ever wanted to get married in the first place. Resigning himself to let SuiLeng have the last word on the matter, James continued telling the story on how he met Father Martin.

"When I first met Father Martin, I was in Saint Ambrosia Church in the back pew closest to the confessional, just staring at the ceiling when he approached. He told me that confessions were over for the evening, but he could take the time to hear mine if that would help, as he assumed that I was in distress and needed someone to talk to. Actually, I did want to talk to someone about what I had done. Upon hearing this, Father Martin thought it best to have the dialogue be under the protection of a confession."

"I told Father Martin that I had killed — that I had become a killer, a vigilante again. He was very upset with me, lecturing me about the sinfulness of taking God's work into my own hands. I countered with a factual account of the inconsistencies between the Old Testament and the New Testament. Realizing that he wasn't dealing with a theological neophyte, he argued with me for almost an hour before I got around to telling him why I had killed again. I told him the story about Mrs. Murphy and her son."

"She was the gentle old woman that I told you about who lived in our neighborhood in Florida; she actually walked past my house several times a week to go to Albertson's food store. I helped carry her groceries home whenever I saw that she had overdone it. She was a believer in fresh vegetables, meat, and fruit; she wouldn't eat any perishable food two days after she bought it. When I read in the paper that she had been severely beaten, was still unconscious and in critical condition, I went to visit her, but I wasn't allowed to see her without family permission. Approaching her son on the matter, he was so obnoxious about it that I became suspicious. For close to a week, I watched all the doctors that worked there. When I saw a bald, large framed, very fit doctor who matched my build, I decided to politely ask if I could borrow his badge, but the conversation did not go well. I didn't want to hurt him at all, but he was so strong that I ended up breaking his jaw to knock him out, which I felt terrible about, but I had to talk to Mrs. Murphy; so, I gently laid him in his car and locked all the doors."

"A few years later, I anonymously donated quite a large

sum of money on his behalf; he told the newspapers that he really had no clue who the mystery benefactor was, but he was ecstatic to have his favorite charity benefit in this manner. This would not be the last time that I associated with this particular doctor, but that is another story."

"My god, James, your life is so convoluted. It's like a jigsaw puzzle."

"SuiLeng, I have come to believe in my lifetime that there is fate, desire, and opportunity, and they are all connected." SuiLeng nodded her head, and James continued.

"From a distance, I knew that I could emulate the doctor's walk and mannerisms, and skin color was no issue; so, I waited until only one nurse was at the nurse's station, then I picked up an empty chart and walked right past her without any acknowledgement at all. As soon as I entered Mrs. Murphy's room, I could feel the intense mental and physical pain within her. Slowly picking up her hand, I knew that she was about to die. We connected for just an instant; she instinctively opened her eyes, and I saw all that I needed to see. She died at peace knowing, at some level in her subconscious mind, that she had told her story to someone."

"She and her son had gotten into a bitter argument over her will earlier on the day that she was beaten. Her son returned late at night, broke an outside window to gain entrance to her house, and then literally beat her to near-death. Before she was unconscious, he had made it a point to let her know who was attacking her. Quite a son, huh. Wearing gloves and boot covers, he took all the Sterling silverware, Hummel's, and cash that he could find in her house to make it look like a professional robbery. Later when I paid him a personal visit, he eventually told me the complete story, as well as the exact location of the canals that he had tossed all of her valuables into."

"However, before I could spend quality time with him, I had to endure watching the smug bastard cry at his mother's wake and funeral when his two sisters flew into town to pay their respect. A few weeks after his family left town, the police found that he had suffered the same fate as his mother. All the items stolen from his mother's house were lying around the chair that he was in, and his mother's will was in his hands. The police never found his killer, but they surmised that the son had arranged the burglary and death of his mother, and had been a little too coy with his accomplices."

"Father Martin was moved by my story, having read the newspaper reports about Mrs. Murphy and the speculation surrounding her son. He remembered thinking that this was such a tragic story for the community to endure. Nonetheless, he was persistent that vengeance and judgment was for God alone; no mortal person had the right to judge another. I reminded Father Martin that the courts of law did this all the time; they judge people for their crimes, and sentence them according to the facts, and I remembered espousing that if this process is done honestly and correctly, then I did not see why the Creator would have an issue with me doing it. I can recall Father Martin's exact words on the matter."

In a very terse, stern voice, Father Martin said, "The Creator has a problem with it because every living creature with a soul has a right to confess and be forgiven for their sins right up to their very last breath, and no one, and I mean absolutely no one, has the right to remove the opportunity for forgiveness from another person's life; such an action is tantamount to murder, even if the person in question has murdered themselves."

"At that moment, it felt like a universal truth had been revealed to me. No one had ever so precisely captured the essence of the argument against capital punishment as Father Martin had. I was impressed, and for once I had to admit that I could not argue against the logic of his statement. But this is precisely why I was sitting in the back of a church in the first place; I needed to know if anyone could offer a different viewpoint other than the one that I had. At that moment, I thought that perhaps my point-of-view had been biased because I had no concept or vision of a life after this one. Things were therefore very black and white; if a person was kind, then kindness should be returned to them, and if a person killed, then death should be the next thing they experience."

"Father Martin then wondered why my own simple rules of life didn't also apply to me. I am sure that he thought he had me there. This was a question that was actually easy to answer; it had been asked of me many times before. The answer was simple: I was absolutely confident that the men I killed were completely evil, for there was not one ounce of remorse or doubt in them when they had killed. The only thing that they were sorry for was that they had been caught and were about to be executed for their crimes. I revealed to Father Martin that I could see into each creature, and know them completely. Being skeptical, he stated that only God could see into a person's soul and tell the truth of their actions. Suggesting that we stop tonight's conversation with a prayer for my soul, it was at that moment when I hit him with the bombshell: I was born hundreds of years ago without a soul, and although I was certainly not a god, I could evolve to have the strength of one. Even one of these statements would seem ludicrous; however, when you throw all these thoughts together and say them with conviction, the outcome or reaction is overwhelming. Father Martin was dumbfounded; he offered to converse with me as often as I would like to validate my statements further."

"A week after our first impromptu meeting, we settled upon a schedule that suited both of us. I would visit Father Martin after night vespers. Then, we would either walk several miles to Deerfield Beach, or walk down Federal Highway, or sit in the rectory common area and converse. It took nearly three weeks of visits for me to tell Father Martin a capsule version of my life. From the look on his face, I could tell that he wasn't buying my life history. I remember making a sarcastic remark that I have a doubting Thomas in my midst and that perhaps a demonstration would help."

"In the Church's common area was a statue of Mother Mary on a marble base. Asking Father Martin how much he thought the statue weighed, he guessed around a ton. Walking over to the stature, I squatted, lifted it off the marble base and set it on the grass beside me. Before he could utter a word, I lifted it back up and placed it where it was. He noticed that I wasn't breathing hard or sweating one bit. Approaching me, he asked me to tell him what his soul looked like. I told him that it was strong, but the tree that best symbolized his soul had many knots; it looked like he had experienced spiritual struggles many times in his life, and although he had overcome them, the scars from the struggle were apparent."

"After that night, I didn't see Father Martin for several weeks; he abruptly left town. When he returned, he wanted me to converse with others in his faith. Now it was my turn to be skeptical and suspicious of his motives. I was torn. I felt like Father Martin and I were becoming friends, but why would he leave town without an explanation? If he didn't believe my story, then that was okay, but why was it important for me to talk with other members of his faith; did I have to convince them too? This situation was becoming unnerving."

"Refusing to meet with anybody for over a week, Father Martin took it upon himself to show up at my house with two other priests. I wanted to give him a piece of my mind, but when I looked into the faces of the other two priests, I remember feeling elated. Never had I seen two mortals so at peace and so closely aligned to their faith; their souls were the most beautiful reflection of life that I had ever seen. The term 'spiritual' was a poor descriptor for these two individuals. Bringing them into my living room, I was actually looking forward to conversing with them, but no one said a word; they all just sat there and stared at me for several minutes. I kept looking back and forth at them and at Father Martin."

"To break the ice, I was about to ask if anyone wanted something to drink, when one of them turned to Father Martin and said that they all could go now. Talking right in front of me, they agreed that I had no soul, but they also said that I was not evil and that I did not have to be destroyed. Well, I was certainly glad to hear that; I am sure that I gave Father Martin a derisive expression as they all piled out my front door. I had no clue that I was being evaluated, and I didn't like it one bit. Father Martin hastily apologized, mumbled something about needing to know, and that he would be getting in touch with me soon."

"Turns out the Church was quite intrigued with me and thought it was a good idea for Father Martin to continue keeping tabs on me. Although I pouted for a while after this, I found that I missed being with Father Martin; so, we met away from the rectory for a couple of months. It was during this time that I told him that I thought I knew what I was, and how I could evolve."

SuiLeng was also intrigued. "James, I knew that you had the aura of an immortal when I first met you, but I always thought that you weren't quite sure what you were?"

"At birth I knew what I was, but so many years have passed since then that doubt has crept in. When we reach Penang and see certain people, I will reconfirm the information that I was born with, but now that we are in danger, I need to tell you what I believe I am, and how I plan on protecting our family."

James reached over and whispered into SuiLeng's ear for several minutes; for the casual observer, it looked they were having an intimate adult conversation.

"Are you sure that is what you are? In all of history, I only thought that Gorgon women, like Medusa, existed as myths. I have never read any literature about Guardians or Gorgon men."

"Actually, one of the first written stories is about men of my kind."

"Nearly everyone has studied that story in school, James. It's just about mankind's fear of being mortal and their longing for immortality; I don't see how the story of Gilgamesh and Enkidu parallels your life."

"Well, the parallel is that both of them possessed incredible strength, strength that gave them the arrogance to challenge the gods themselves. And Enkidu was befriended by the animals while he was pure, before he was seduced by a woman. They trusted him up to that point. I read a text at the turn of the century that stated they were fraternal brothers who had not yet evolved when they first met, which is why they didn't know they were brothers at that point in time. It is very rare for males in our species to be born in the same time period."

"You are losing me again, James. What text did you read?"

"That's another really long story. Let's wait on that one."

Rolling her eyes, "Is there any story that isn't long?"

James ignored her comment. "Imprinted in my brain is the knowledge or the thought that men of my kind are born as fraternal twins; however, we can never link or truly know of one another's existence until one of us evolves, and then we instantly become bonded and see each other. So if I am right about what I am, then I will see my brother after I evolve. The men of our kind can evolve four times, and the woman only evolve three times. And before I hear any sarcastic remarks about that, the women of our race are physically much stronger than men when they are born; men have to evolve one level before they exceed a woman's strength at birth. The danger in evolving for the men is that each level requires them to master intense physical pain, along with the mental panic associated with overloaded sensory inputs to their conscious mind. If a host can't handle it, then they will die in a matter of days. Turns out that women of our kind are better suited for handling the mental aspects of evolving, along with the physical pain."

"Oh, you mean to tell me that women in your race are better suited for handling pain and having more mental discipline than men? All you guys are such babies—when you get sick, or even have a simple headache, you whine and whine. It is a wonder that you stay focused enough to accomplish anything at all."

"Well, we must have some redeeming features; you women still seek our companionship."

"James, any redeeming feature that men have is highly overrated; women only stay with men because they believe that they will change them someday. That is our weakness I think. We should cut our losses sooner than we do."

"And what about love?" inquired James.

"Another highly overrated emotion. Now continue the story please; we only have five more hours of layover left before we have to fly to Singapore. I hope that you're done with this story by then."

"So you're not worried about my safety when I evolve?"

"No, your will is up to date, right?" SuiLeng definitely had that playful look in her eyes. "Will you get better looking when you evolve? Or, perhaps you'll have more endurance and stay stiffer longer—now that would be an improvement."

James could only smile; she was so small yet so tough, and you never knew what she was going to say. In a very serious tone, James stated that he thought both might happen: his physical features would change slightly, his strength would grow dramatically, and he was pretty sure that he would have more physical control of his body along with an enhanced mental ability to see into people. Presently, he could smell an enemy in the same room with him. After he evolved, he thought that he might be able to sense an enemy quite a distance away. The one concern he had was that when he changed, he would be different, and he wasn't sure how that would affect them. On top of that, the bond to his brother would add complexity to existing relationships.

Sensing his doubt, SuiLeng reached over for his hand. Speaking from her heart, she said, "I believe in you. Do what you think is right for our family, but please be careful. I don't know if I can take losing another husband, but I know I would never survive if anything happened to my children."

After pausing, she continued speaking again. "My only

concern is why Father Martin fears what will happen when you evolve. Does he know something that you don't know?"

"I don't know what he fears. He certainly knows that my powers will be enhanced. Perhaps he is concerned that I won't be able to handle it. Perhaps he fears that the Church will become nervous and declare me unfit for this world—something that must be eradicated. I hope that it does not come to that because that would force me to take more drastic steps; I would need to evolve faster than is prudent."

"What do you become when you evolve a second time?"

James looked away as he answered, "Something that neither of us would be ready for right now."

Chapter 16

THE RETURN HOME

Islamic Year: 1377 AH   *1958 AD*

    After the last meeting in Mr. Jiling's office, the weeks and months went by without any further altercations. John Parella, Sr. said a heartfelt goodbye to Jahleel and many other close work associates. Out of courtesy, Mr. Jiling shook John's hand and wished him well when he left, but his words were betrayed by the banal look on his face.

    On the way to Riyadh, John noted the smells and sounds of the desert and its people one last time, quietly saying goodbye as he prepared for a long set of commercial flights that would take him back to New York, then onto Phildadelphia.

    Before his plane departed for Frankfurt, John was surprised by a visit from the Minister and his entourage of guards. Standing up to greet him, John and the Minister exchanged formal greetings, and then the Minister gave John the sign to sit down. They were noticeably comfortable in each other's presence, appearing as if they had been friends since childhood. The Minister spoke first.

    "Mr. Parella, many Westerners have come to our country.

While they are courteous and appear on the outside to understand our culture, they only do so because it is a necessary business obligation on their part in order to obtain profits for their companies. Deep inside, they have no real respect for our way of life or our Islamic religion. But you are different; you have openly shared knowledge with us. You have toiled and sweated beside us, you have helped us through our failures, and you have joyfully celebrated our successes. You have eaten with us; you have treated us as equals, and along the way you have absorbed some of our way of life. Of all the things that I could say to you, perhaps the most meaningful is that you have earned our respect, and that compliment is one that we do not take lightly."

John was humbled by the Minister's remarks. Of all the gifts that one man can bestow upon another, this was the one that he treasured the most.

"I am honored to have been part of the legacy that you and the King are creating," John replied, smiling.

"Ah, a man of few words. You are indeed a pleasure to be with. I wish that Allah had chosen a path for us that would have allowed us to share more personal time together. But it does appear that Allah may have given us common ground to continue along, even though we may never see each other again in our lifetimes. The King and I have mulled this over a great deal during the last several months, and we have decided that an integral part of the knowledge that we have been blessed to receive must be shared with others who are outside our faith. Since you have proven yourself as one who can be trusted, I want you to accept this satchel that contains translated copies of several texts plus a personal letter from me, which you can read on the plane. But for now, I want to say goodbye and wish you and your family well."

Standing and shaking the Minister's right hand firmly, John looked at the Minister one last time as they said their formal goodbyes in Arabic.

An hour into the flight, John opened the brown leather satchel and removed the sealed envelope. Inside were several pages of a handwritten letter.

Dear Mr. Parella,

By now, you are aboard the plane and starting your long journey home. In writing this letter, I had to pause and reflect on the religious and secular beliefs that made us, Easterners and Westerners, apprehensive of one another in past centuries. In those times, there was no real respect for one another; therefore, there was no pathway to earn each other's trust, and without trust, there is no basis for any type of relationship. Yet, due to your actions over the last five years, we have learned to trust one another at a fundamental level – a level that will transcend the years that will grow between us. A level which allows our faith in one another never to be shaken, even when that faith is tested by outside forces. I pray to Allah that He gives you the strength to consider what will be asked of you in this letter and to follow the course of action laid out before all of us in this instance. As you will see, with the sharing of great knowledge comes the great responsibility to act on that knowledge.

The magnitude of the information that has been presented to us is unquestionably monumental; while some parts of it are disturbing, other parts are wonderful, and I want to share that part with you now. Not too far into the future, scientists will tell the world that the Universe was created eons ago from a single explosion of concentrated matter that would easily fit in the palm of your hand. They will even be able to tell the world what the early Universe looked like using Cosmic Microwave Background information, and they will also say that, when the Universe cooled down from its fiery birth, the physical laws that define and govern all the suns and planets were created. They will then vigorously debate whether the hand of Allah was present at the beginning of the Universe. This will once again pit scientific and religious organizations against one another. Some scientists will argue that dark unseen matter and energy, once studied, will answer many mysteries of the Universe. Religious organizations and enlightened, pragmatic scientists who are humbled by the beauty and glory of the Universe will use science to help in this argument. They will point out that at the birth of the Universe, more matter than anti-matter was present, and that such an unbalanced equation could only exist for a small fraction of time. It could not be maintained over billions of years; therefore, an intervention had to occur.[18] Yes, Mr. Parella, let me leave no doubt – the information revealed to us confirms, without question, that Allah intervened and created the Universe, and that Creation just does not randomly transform itself without will – without thought. When He created the Universe, Allah absorbed enough anti-matter with his own energy to allow the skies, the planets, and the heavens to exist. In addition, it will be discovered that the Universe is still expanding and will not contract upon itself. The force doing this cannot be explained by scientists, yet such a force is ever present in our Universe. Only one explanation fits the facts, when all other explanations are removed–Allah exists and wills the Universe to his plan.[19]

Furthermore, it is clear in this Creation that Allah gave of Himself, and that he permeates every rock, tree, and particle of nature throughout the Universe. All life in this world and this Universe are part of Allah, whether or not they believe in Him. To sense Allah, a person only has to look inside themselves and listen to their conscience–to their soul. While our faiths have always taught us that this is so, and all life around us confirms this, it is glorious to receive this additional confirmation. I wish that I could share this moment with you, to look upon your face and see the joy that fills your heart now as it did mine. Savor this moment, and let it sustain you for a long time to come.

Mr. Parella, the King and I have a distinct advantage over you for having spent years reviewing, discussing, and diagnosing subtleties in regards to this information, but let us think about it for a moment. What are the thoughts that older people worry about as they approach the end of their time? The answer is that they wonder how immortal the memory of them will be. They will wonder if they will be remembered for the power that they had, and the elements of social change that they initiated. They wonder if the things that they created in their lifetime (a family, architecture, art, or literature) will survive the test of time. For those that pursued their dreams, they will take solace in a lifetime of work. If they decided to raise a family, then they will take comfort in seeing their family happy, seeing their children be healthy and grow up to be mature, moral people that are capable of taking care of themselves and their families. However, those people who lived in fear of taking a risk and did not pursue their inner dreams will chastise and torture themselves at the end of their life for not trying; they will most likely become bitter and sad during their lifetime.

Now let's think of Allah. Already, He is immortal. Already, He has power beyond human comprehension – so what would He choose to spend His time doing? What risks would He want to take? What would make Him happy or sad? The answer is simple: Allah is a master artist; He would spend time creating an endless, ever-evolving masterpiece. He would take the risk of further creating life in His own image and allowing that life to grow and make its own decisions. He would share their joys and successes, and He would equally feel the pain and terror of those children that sin and from those that suffer from in-decision.

John put the letter down for a few minutes and thought about the words that he had just read. He had always believed that there was a God. He heard many eloquent arguments on why God didn't exist over the years; two World Wars in a span of forty years had shaken most people's faith. But whenever he felt troubled, he would merely gaze into the night sky, marvel at the abundant stars and realize that he was part of something wonderful—something that had to have purpose and thought. His intuition and common sense had always told him that this was true. Now he knew for sure, and the Minister was right: he was overwhelmed with joy. He was almost afraid to continue reading the letter, for how could any other news be more compelling than what he had just learned.

I know that you are still amazed at what you have been told so far, but even more startling is the information that Allah has re-built and re-created the Universe several times before. At times, He has merely started new work on old foundations, much like new cities being built on top of ancient ones. However, several translations also allude to the need to totally start anew. We do not, at this point, clearly understand the reasons for all previous re-creations of the Universe, but there are volumes of texts that still have not been deciphered; perhaps, in time, we will learn more and be able to find these answers.

Nevertheless, let's not dwell on what we do not know; there are four profound pieces of information that we have uncovered over 53 years of study.

First, Allah creates life forms – not machines. He wants life that can think, experiment, learn from mistakes, dream, and envision a future that does not yet exist. This is perhaps what makes His masterpieces so interesting. When He created perfect life forms before and imbued them with all the knowledge that they needed to live orderly, moral lives and maintain the Universe, these life forms never took great risks. They never aspired for physical or spiritual zeniths. They were somewhat complacent; so, in this one instance, He absorbed them spiritually and started over.

Second, Allah exists in the past, present and future simultaneously; therefore, He sees all possible outcomes from each decision that is made.[20]

Third, because Allah is everywhere at once, time for Him is not a linear process or a line of sequential events that happen one after the other. Time is really only a human concept, and the Universe, under Allah, is not governed by this principle, which means events in history can be changed by one such as Allah.[21]

Now before you panic, Mr. Parella, Allah does not expect you or I to manage the decision making of all life over all time, nor manage the nuances of events in a particular time. We have a small, focused role in helping this world, which is one of Allah's special places. Our role is to be ready if any Guardians reveal themselves in our lifetime and make the decision to evolve. This will be the primary signal that mankind is failing in its overall mission. These beings are capable of performing great deeds for humanity and this world, or they can mercilessly eradicate all ill will and rule this world with a taunt iron fist.

Four, because Allah exists, evil and its children also exist. Evil caused tens of millions of lives to be lost in several world wars, and in the aftermath of world wars in just this century alone. I do not want to dwell on the evil in this world. Others will keep a vigilant watch on that situation, and although evil has the insatiable dreams that every dictator has, its lust is solely for this world. The Universe will not live or die by what it does in this world alone. However, I must caution you to teach your children never to accept its help, no matter how desperate things seem at the moment. Remember, evil will only provide help when events are in its favor. Evil will always have hidden agendas.

For what will be asked of you and your children, the events over the next 140 years need to be explained to you. Neither you nor your children will be able to change these events, but you must be aware of them so that you respond to them accordingly. As you might expect, Saudi Arabia will continue to grow; it will become a political force in the world by the end of this century. In fact, the Saudi Arabian Government and the American Government will form close relationships, and Saudi Arabia will own hundreds of billions of dollars in US assets. However, by the end of the 21st century, new sources of energy will exist on a massive scale: solar power, wind farms, compressed and liquified natural gas engines as well as hybrid and electric automobiles that run on advanced chemistries with improved gravimetric energy density, and cycle life. Therefore, the influence that Saudi Arabia had previously exercised over the world will diminish. The same will be true of America.

For America, the cost of new wars just beyond the end of this century will drain your coffers. However, it is Wall Street and the national and international corporate tax structure that will push American Industry into a death spiral, defeating America from within. In the pursuit of higher quarterly earnings required by Wall Street, America will finally outsource a critical mass of manufacturing and engineering jobs to Asia. The result of all this will lead to a declining innovation infrastructure in the United States, and a staggering ever-increasing annual trade deficit with China. Asia and China will start to turn out more scientists, engineers and patents overall than the United States, such that the ingenuity fueling America's growth in the past will now be controlled by others. America will move from an industrial society to a service society; entrepreneurship will not be the norm. The result of all this will be, for the first time in America's history, your children and their children, unless very highly educated, will not see a better life than their parents, and given the exponential increasing cost of higher education, America will relinquish its role as the world's superpower to China a hundred years from now, just as Britain previously relinquished that role to America.

Again, you cannot change these events, but you must be aware of them. I have detailed the financial investments and decisions that you need to make over time so that you can insulate your family from the effects of these events in order to pursue the other work outlined in this letter.

For the next part of this letter, I sincerely apologize for what we will ask you to do, especially with regards to your children. Every day for the last three months, I have prayed to Allah that we have interpreted all the documents correctly, and the answer always comes back the same.

As John read the next few pages, his whole body shook. Putting the letter aside, he placed his hands over his eyes and began to cry. He realized the trouble that the world was in and the agony that Abraham felt the moment after the Angels asked him to sacrifice his son to God; such was the terror in his heart right now. A passenger behind him placed a hand on his shoulder and asked if he was alright. John composed himself, meekly replying that he was just happy to be finally going home. Forty minutes later, he picked up the letter again.

I know what you are going through right now; knowing what you now know, the burden of taking action or doing nothing has been clearly placed on your shoulders. The guilt that you will suffer in your lifetime by either decision that you make will be almost unbearable. Again, I pray to Allah that He gives you the strength to make the right decision. Please take this small measure of solace: if you decide to act, then you will only have to choose one of your children to suffer this fate. Once that decision is made, events will naturally unfold after that. In addition, I want you to know that you and your family for all generations to come will be under the protection of the Royal family; you do not have to ask how it will be done, rest assured that it will be so.

John finished the letter, folded it up, and put it back in the satchel, which he placed in the empty seat beside him. With his hand gripping the satchel, sleep never came to him for the entire journey home as he thought about the sacrifice that one of his sons would have to make. In fact, from this moment onward, John Parella, Sr.'s dreams, and his children's dreams would always create anguish for him. From this point onward, he would never know if their dreams were portents of an impending doom in the future, or harmless blends of daily life.

Chapter 17

HOTEL MONTGOMERY, 1983

Hotel Montgomery, 1983 6:45 AM

Mr. Moressy walked up to the front desk to chat with Bob and Phil. "The coffee smells real good this morning, boys."

"Just ground up the beans myself and brewed 'em; you going to have some coffee this morning, Mr. Moressy, before you go out for your walk?" asked Bob.

"No, my prostate is still acting up; got to take care of these things at my age."

Bob and Phil looked at one another, but before they could prepare a playful retort to such a blatant lie, they all simultaneously turned their attention to the lady who had just entered the hotel. Barely over five feet, she was an elegant southern belle of forty-five plus years with a dainty gait, blond bouffant hair, a peaches and crème complexion, and size six high heel shoes.

"Gentlemen, I was walking by your hotel this morning, and the Florentine exterior caught my attention. I just had to come back and take a peek inside, and after seeing how beautiful it is in here, I am glad that I did. My name is Miss Marla."

Her eyes were greeted by the pink hue of marble floors, hand carved walnut panels that flowed up to a two story height, a 22 carat gold and crystal chandelier in the main lobby, and the breathtaking double flight of stairs that lead to the second floor, with each stairway outlining an expansive atrium where guests leisurely socialized.

Phil walked around the front desk to introduce himself and personally greet Miss Marla, while proceeding to tell her a little bit about the hotel.

"This hotel has two hundred and forty-two rooms, with additional executive suites on the third floor, and several penthouse rooms on the fourth floor; many of our guests choose to stay here year round. The atrium and arbor area beyond is just one of the features of this hotel's charm. My brother Bob and I helped construct it nearly twenty years ago. We brought ambiance from some of finest hotels that we stayed at and added some of our own. Would you like me to show you around? "

"Yes, that would be very nice, Phil. You know gentlemen, I do think that I am going to enjoy staying here a while."

―――∞―――

Hotel Montgomery, 10 years later 1993　　　　　　*6:45 AM*

Bob and Phil were busy preparing the front desk. Their daily routine emulated a pattern that they had repeated a thousand times before.

Each of them mentally noted that Mr. Moressy had not come down to the lobby yet for his daily walk. Bob commented to Phil that he was getting worried about him. Lately, he seemed preoccupied; his quick wit and sarcastic banter was replaced by silence and sullen periods of deep thought, as though he was carrying heavy emotional burdens. All enquiries into his apparent troubles were answered with an apology for drifting off again.

"You know Bob, if he doesn't come down soon, I'm going to check up on him."

"Good idea. You know, well…oh, hello sir. I'm sorry, I didn't see you come in."

The stranger before them was wearing a green weathered London Fog coat and carrying a worn, brown leather satchel. Unshaven, looking beleaguered and weary, this person appeared to have traveled a great distance with little or no sleep.

"I would like a room for three days if you have one."

"Why yes, sir, we do. Please sign the register, and we will get you settled straight away," replied Bob.

"I see you are a Mr. John Parella, Senior, is that the correct pronunciation?"

"Yes, it is."

"Well, I have a message for you," Phil began. "Miss Marla will meet you for breakfast at 7:30 AM sharp."

"Good. May I also enquire if a Mr. Moressy is staying here?"

"Why yes, sir, he is, but he has not come down yet."

"Well, I don't want to disturb him; I'll catch up with him later."

Chapter 18

VOICES

Dr. Duhring glanced one more time at Stephen and Evan just before she closed her office door. Her senses told her that they were acting out of character, but perhaps she was overreacting to their behavior. She was on edge from the morning news broadcast of the press conference at the Clinic and the public humiliation that Dr. Ashe had to endure, plus the pent-up anxiety over whether Dr. Amello would help her or not. As she turned around to face him and John Parella, Jr., she saw that both men were staring at her intently. It was a good thing that she had taken a run this morning to burn off excess tension; from the looks on their faces, her patience and interpersonal skills would be thoroughly tested today.

"Dr. Amello, this is John Parella, Jr.; he is a very accomplished business person and inventor in his own right, who has published articles in many scientific trade journals, and he just needs a bit of our help to get back on his feet again."

John, sitting in front of Dr. Duhring's desk, stood up to shake hands with Dr. Amello.

Dr. Duhring continued the introductions. "John, Dr. Peter Amello is a very distinguished member of the staff here at the Institute. He is world renowned in hypnotherapy, having published eighty articles and fourteen books on the subject, while also lecturing at many universities around the world. He has a lovely wife and three gorgeous children, and yet he still manages to find the time to have an active practice here at the Institute. He is a gem, and since I have been here at the Institute, I can tell you that he commands the respect of everyone on the staff."

John openly nodded his approval of Dr. Amello's credentials; turning his head toward Dr. Duhring, he smiled, seeming pleased. The point was captured and duly noted by Dr. Duhring; pausing for a half-second, she continued.

"John, one forte of Dr. Amello's is in an auto-questioning technique and Indirect Hypnotic permissive techniques; several of his books delve into this subject."

"Oh, really? Well, I'm pretty familiar with auto-questioning. Dr. Ashe had me doing this for the last four months; he was hoping that if I took ownership of asking my own subconscious mind about my weight problems and depressive moods that I would gain more insight into myself. I liked the idea; so, I kept a journal of all the questions and answers that I asked."

Somewhat surprised, Dr. Duhring replied, "John, Dr. Ashe never indicated this method of therapy in any of his case notes."

"Well, Doctor Duhring, it was something that we were doing on the side. He wanted to try something different. We often worked outside his office; you know, going for long walks around the grounds when the weather permitted it. I really liked this approach, because it felt personal instead of clinical."

"I was wondering about that," said Dr. Amello. "The Clinic has several skilled staff members in hypnotic techniques; Dr. Ashe had at least twenty-four hours of course-work under my tutelage at the University of Pennsylvania. What techniques did he have you use for auto questioning?"

"He called it the Chevreul Pendulum or something like that. Anyway, I drew a circle on a large piece of paper and divided it into six slices of a pie, so to speak. Dr. Ashe and I shared a joy in eating food; so, he would often use food analogies to explain concepts to me. Anyway, I tied my wedding ring to a ten inch string—I didn't have any other use for it now that I am divorced, and it felt good to use it for something that might help me. I would set my left elbow steadily on the table while holding the string to my wedding ring in my left hand, and position the ring over the center of the circle on the paper. It took me quite a while just to find out which slices of the pie meant yes, no, maybe, don't want to answer, rephrase the question, and escape. Then I was able to ask myself lots of questions."[22]

"Okay," responded Dr. Amello. "So how did you do?"

"Well, at first it was hard, you know, to try and think of the right questions to ask in order to learn about myself, but after a few months, I got good at it. I began to realize that my subconscious was like a whole other person; when it got tired, it was time to stop, but I, or we, were able to build up our endurance for doing this. Sometimes, we could continue this for a few hours."

Dr. Amello glanced at Dr. Duhring for a split second; he was concerned with the use of the word 'we' that John used to describe himself and his subconscious. Noting Dr. Duhring's non-verbal acknowledgement, he asked a different question.

"Excellent John, and did you and Dr. Ashe discuss what you learned about yourself?"

"Yes, but I was a bit embarrassed at my dysfunctions; how they started, and why they were so firmly established in my subconscious mind. However, Dr. Ashe wasn't one for trying to find out why a dysfunction existed. Since the problem was already there, he wanted me to find out what daily events triggered my reactions, depression and eating binges so that we could move into suggestive therapy to alter my behaviors. But none of the suggestive therapy that we engaged in took hold."

"Mr. Parella, I must say that Dr. Ashe's approach is a valid technique, and he was a darn good psychiatrist in my opinion;

so, I am quite surprised that some progress wasn't made over the period of time that you mentioned. Did Dr. Ashe ever give an indication to you on why your progress was so slow?"

"Not until the end there, just a few days before I jumped off the wall. Dr. Ashe surmised that my subconscious mind had a built-in blocking mechanism like password protected files on a computer; it wasn't going to allow me to get better. He also indicated that he was getting a bit flustered."

Dr. Duhring interrupted, "John that does not sound like Dr. Ashe, and I'm troubled that none of this is in any case notes or recordings. Are you sure that you are properly conveying the context of your dialogues?"

"I am not making this up. If you get my journal from my room at the Clinic, then you can verify what I just said!" John was beginning to get indignant and loud.

Dr. Amello thought about John's words for a few seconds, and then he started to ask more direct questions.

"John, what else can you tell us about the day that you and Dr. Ashe had that discussion? What was going through your mind before the session?"

"Well, I was really tired and cranky that day. I barely got any sleep the night before. For weeks, I kept having the same dream over and over again. It was driving me crazy, which causes a lot of anxiety, then I eat a lot of food even though I'm not hungry, which then gets me really depressed. I was a basket case by the time my session with Dr. Ashe started. And then when I get like this, I start thinking of all the time spent at the Clinic, and then I get really pissed off because my problems aren't getting resolved. Plus, I started thinking that Dr. Junger had given up on me and pawned me off on Dr. Ashe during the last year there. I know that I'm rambling, but all these thoughts were on my mind when I talked with Dr. Ashe that day."

"Did you ever share your recurring dreams with Dr. Ashe?"

"Yes, we discussed it several times, and I would prefer not to have to repeat it again here."

Dr. Amello took John's answer in stride; he possessed a vast repertoire of skills acquired over the years in helping patients elicit their deepest fears and concerns.

"John, that's fine; you don't have to share the dream with us. But from what I gathered, you came to that particular session with Dr. Ashe tired, unnerved by this recurring dream, and how your conscious mind and subconscious mind deals with stressful situations like this. On top of that, since you got depressed over the whole situation, this caused you to vent your frustration over not making any real progress with Dr. Ashe at the Clinic. Did you verbally share all these emotions with him at this session, or was all this conveyed by your attitude?"

"Initially, it was my attitude and short answers to his questions, which actually caused him to give me a piece of his mind that day."

"Really. What did he say to you?" inquired Dr. Amello, surprised yet interested.

"Well, after putting up with my abrupt-then-lackadaisical manner for most of the meeting, he chastised me for having poor overall self-discipline. We had been over my eating disorders and the depression that it caused for months, and we discovered that my subconscious mind equates food with comfort and security, which is why I eat when I am nervous or stressed. We had actually conquered the eating disorder even though I was still having these dreams; so, he got upset when I relapsed. I must have eaten eight cinnamon rolls on top of breakfast and lunch before I got to his office."

"John, did anything else happen?"

"Aw, geez...well, a few days after my session with Dr. Ashe, I got into one hell of an argument with Mr. Woodrow in room 214, which played out for the entire dining room to hear. He didn't like my appearance and attitude, either; he was tired of my wrinkled clothes, unshaven face, and sarcastic conversation at the evening meals. One thing lead to another and instead of just walking away, I lambasted him on his nagging, self-righteous behavior, and then I hit him right between the eyes when I stated that he probably made his wife's life a living hell while they were together. His wife died of cancer a few years back, and it was painful for him from what I heard. I felt awful, but I couldn't apologize quickly enough. The impact was devastating. He broke down right there at the dinner table, and couldn't stop crying. It was a mess, and, if looks could kill, the entire table would have hung me on the spot."

Hesitantly, Dr. Amello asked, "So, you think this event triggered your eating disorder?"

"Well, not entirely. My dream that night keep playing over and over again from start to finish. It was like a tape that kept rewinding at the end of the movie, but the more that it played the slower and louder the words became. Movements were very exaggerated, and that never happened to me before. I woke up startled; I was sweating so badly that you might have thought that I just went swimming. It was really intense, and that was the first time that my dreams really scared me."

Dr. Duhring noticeably perked up at this response and leaned forward, "John, thinking back on it now, what do you think scared you the most about this dream sequence?"

"I don't know," John mumbled; his words barely audible.

This is where Dr. Duhring had lost John in all the previous sessions that she had with him. Just as he was about to share a revealing bit of information, he would look at the floor and shut down. She glanced at Dr. Amello, conveying a sense of urgency to salvage the situation. Nodding his head in response, he turned his attention to John, knowing that he had to get John out of the mood that he had just entered, or this session, and perhaps all future sessions, would bear little results.

"John, how about a cup of tea and a word game?" said Dr. Amello sprightly.

John's head snapped right up in reply to such a ridiculous idea. "What?"

"You heard me, let's have a relaxing cup of tea and try a

word game. I am going to—"

"A word game?" John was getting irritated again. "We aren't on a vacation here, playing twenty questions to pass the time. My goodness."

"Then what are we doing here?" responded Dr. Amello.

"Well, we're trying to, you know...help me by, uh, assessing my state of mind, and…"

Dr. Amello and Dr. Duhring stayed quiet and just stared at John for close to eight seconds. He continued his stammering to break the silence. "Fine, you're trying to help me. Ok, let's play the word game."

"Okay," Dr. Amello continued. "First though, let me make you a cup of tea; Dr. Duhring has several kinds here, what do you prefer?"

"I like Darjeeling," responded John.

Walking over to the credenza, Dr. Amello said, "In fact, let's all have a cup of tea. I for one have had my fill of coffee this morning." He glanced at Dr. Duhring after emphasizing the word *tea*.

The little jab was not lost on Dr. Duhring; however, she played along. "I'll have a cup of Earl Gray if you don't mind, Doctor."

"And what would each of you like with your tea?"

Dr. Duhring just asked for a little lemon with hers, no sugar. John asked for three Sweet N' Low packages, plus a little milk.

"Wow," replied Dr. Amello. "You always put that much sweetener in your tea?"

"Actually, not before I started therapy. Seems that I acquired the taste for sweetener at the Clinic."

Handing each cup of tea to Dr. Duhring and John, Dr. Amello sat back down with his own cup. "Okay, here is how I would like to play this game. I want you to close your eyes and answer each question with three one word responses; do you understand?"

"Yes, go on."

"Okay, let's get started," said Dr. Amello. "The first word is *rich."*

"Pools, art, loneliness."

"Question: what physically defines a beautiful woman?"

"Lips, hair, figure."

"What mentally defines a beautiful woman?"

"Intelligence, conversation, self-confidence."

"What characteristics define a man that you respect?"

"Honesty, strength, independence."

"What is a mother?"

"Concern, love, understanding."

"What is a father?"

"Strength, protection, fun."

"What causes divorce?"

John opened his eyes and glared at Dr. Amello, then turning his head toward Dr. Duhring. He almost spit the answers out. "Selfishness, ego, stubbornness."

"Why do you love your children?"

John had to pause; tears formed on the corner of his eyes as he closed them again. "New life, beauty, innocence."

"Why do your dreams scare you?"

"I feel helpless, out of control, confused."

"Do your dreams tell you to do things, John?"

"Yes, not always; the recent ones do."

"Is your father or mother in your dreams?"

"Yes, my father."

"Does your father, or any other family member, tell you to do things, John?"

"Yes, my father tells me to listen."

"What role does your father play in your dreams?"

"He always consoles me and comforts me; he tells me that everything will be alright. Even though the things that I need to do seem difficult, he gives me reassurance."

"Who does your father want you to listen to in your dreams?"

"Moressy, mostly."

Dr. Amello paused and looked at Dr. Duhring to get a

read on who Moressy was; she shrugged her shoulders. This momentary pause in questioning caused John to open his eyes again. He gulped down his cup of tea and asked if he could have another. This time Dr. Duhring got up to make it. Dr. Amello was getting through to John, and she didn't want to derail the progress being made. To keep John focused, she asked if he still wanted three Sweet N' Low with his tea. He actually asked for more; to him, the tea was weak but tart. As Dr. Duhring handed John the cup of tea, she noticed that his hands were shaking; concerned she asked if he was alright.

"Yes, I'm fine. The tea will settle me down," replied John.

John slurped the tea down in two gulps, totally oblivious to how hot it was. A few seconds later, he shuttered and shook violently, as if he was having an epileptic seizure, after which his head slumped down toward his chest. As Dr. Amello and Dr. Duhring both simultaneously approached John, his head snapped up, and an older voice with a strong timbre addressed them.

"Doctors, relax, John is fine. I, on the other hand, need some help."

Chapter 19

PREPARING FOR DR. JUNGER

SuiLeng didn't know how to handle James' last answer. It actually scared her that he was nervous about what he could eventually become as he continued to evolve. Knowing him well enough not to press him when he was distraught about a situation, for now, she thought it was best to redirect the conversation.

"James, when did you first meet Dr. Junger?"

"I was in Japan on ship leave. He helped me. I thought that he was actually a good Samaritan at first."

SuiLeng was puzzled. "Ship leave, when did you ever work on a ship?"

"In the late 1870s, I was a freight hopper. Best damn cargo loader and unloader that anyone ever saw."

"What? Are you telling me that Dr. Junger is over a hundred years old?"

"Actually, I have no clue how old he is, but he sure acts like he knows everything."

SuiLeng sat up straight in her chair. "What is he? Is he like you?"

"I don't know exactly what he is, and I sure as hell don't trust anything that he has told me about himself."

Father Martin pulled up to his initial seminary training school in Elkton, Maryland just before noon. As he approached the large complex, he noticed that the years hadn't changed the place much. Cattle were still raised on the grounds; he saw the partial bales of hay dotted across the fields to feed them. This was a morning task that he always enjoyed doing right after 6 AM prayers and right before 7 AM breakfast. In the summertime, the dew and emerging sunlight always gave the pastures a soothing ethereal quality. In the winter, he remembered riding on the back of the hay wagon as Father Paul raced the tractor around the fields, trying to do his best to tip Father Martin off the hay cart without sending the whole wagon over. It was one of the games that they enjoyed playing. At night, hundreds of young hopeful priests in training played pinochle and conversed about seminary life and the way that their families and friends felt about their chosen vocation. It was a beautiful time in his life. The only sad thing to note over the years was that enrollment had tapered off dramatically, and although the place wasn't buzzing with the same zestful energy that hundreds of people tended to give it, the seminary school still had its grandeur and spiritual serenity.

As he should have suspected, an aging Father Paul was standing on the front steps to the three story complex and tapping his watch just as he used to do when Father Martin was more than a few minutes late for vespers or class. Of all the men and clergymen that Father Martin had met in his lifetime, Father Paul was the best role model and mentor that he could have ever had. The man was completely unpretentious and full of integrity, yet he had compassion for other's weaknesses and never gave up on them, even if the person that he was trying to help gave up on themselves for a time. He was a true champion of the teachings of Jesus; if the Catholic Church could just find more people like him, then Father Martin was sure that more young men would choose the Church and its mission as their vocation.

As Father Martin closed his car door, Father Paul spoke. "Well, I see that years of training and exemplary accomplishments all over the world still have not improved your ability to arrive on time for a meeting."

"Oh, c'mon now. I couldn't be more than a few minutes late."

"Try twenty minutes late — and, for your information, Mrs. Johnson makes home-made, dough-wrapped mini-hot-dogs on Tuesdays for lunch, and I will be in a very sour mood if they are all gone by now."

Laughing out loud, Father Martin retorted, "And here I thought that you were still top man at this facility; did they put you out to pasture already?"

"Only top man in spiritual matters, and the obedient, useful members of the Church are never put out to pasture, Father Martin."

"Ouch, I didn't even shake your hand yet, and already we have begun the lecture for today."

"God's work has no vacation time from tutoring; as I last remember, there are still twenty-four hours in a day, or perhaps the clocks in Florida churches are on a different schedule?"

Father Martin conceded. "Okay, okay, let's get you some mini-dogs before they're gone; they must be heavenly."

"Let's put it this way: the one year that I gave them up for Lent was the only time that I ever received any negative feedback from my students and the Bishop."

The two men walked into the large dining hall that had a mechanized tray handling/cleaning system that was built for over three hundred associates, yet only twenty young seminary students were in training at the moment. Father Martin sensed Father Paul's disappointment, but it was a fact of life that the Church was coming to grips with and trying to address. The mini-dogs served with a touch of mustard plus a light oil and vinegar salad made of spinach, endive, cucumber and radishes immediately improved Father Paul's disposition.

After lunch, they stopped by the chapel and walked around the classrooms to note the expensive in-ceiling computer aided projectors that replaced the archaic mylar film projectors they used in Father Martin's time, and to note the state-of-the-art conferencing equipment that had been installed to allow other lecturers from around the world to teach the students. Father Martin complimented Father Paul on the use of modern equipment to enhance the learning experience. With the decline in the number of students, such innovative ideas were required to spread the limited man-power over the globe. The Church almost always had money, but it lacked the people to teach and lead at times.

Father Martin also noted that a few classrooms still had chalk and chalkboards, which was the primary teaching tool in his day. Father Paul was quick to comment that, while chalk and chalkboards were relics of the past, they still had their use. Noting the chagrin on Father Paul's face, Father Martin also felt like a relic stumbling around in the dark in a fast moving world. His body told him that he was getting too old for this stuff, and his brain seemed like it was four software versions behind his adversaries. He would have liked to be a 'Colombo' like police personality; appearing to be slow and dimwitted to all the suspects around him, yet be as sharp as a tack behind the scenes. Father Paul, like a parent to Father Martin, was always able to sense his moods. They went up to Father Paul's office on the second floor in silence.

As they entered Father Paul's office, Father Martin noted that the décor was essentially the same. Hard leather bound books lined the bookshelves on the entire wall behind the desk. A new coat of bright yellow paint was on the other three walls, and although the drapes around the two windows had finally been changed, the same gnarled, solid oak chairs still sat in front of Father Paul's desk. It was good to see that some things never changed. There wasn't a speck of dust anywhere in the room; it was still a bright, cheery, warm, and friendly room, which was very reflective of Father Paul's personality.

Father Paul closed the door behind them, and then proceeded to walk around his desk and sit in his chair. This gave a very formal setting to what Father Martin had hoped would be an informal discussion, where they would sit in the two oak chairs in front of his desk and chat as they used to when Father Martin had troubles in the past and had sought out Father Paul's advice.

"So Father Martin, when you called me a few days ago, you seemed a bit distraught. You wanted to meet to seek counseling on matters involving your latest work and a growing trepidation that you might be inadequate to handle all the things going on at once."

Amazed, Father Martin said, "You got all that out of our three minute conversation."

"It's what you didn't say on the phone and what you just confirmed now, with your body language, that I got out of our brief conversation a few days ago."

The tone from Father Paul was too formal. Father Martin was at a momentary loss for words, wondering if he had made a mistake in coming here for advice, but he needed to confide in someone. Having previously threatened to go solo on many assignments in the past, he had never done that until now, always considering himself a mature and honest person, which was what his reputation was built on.

"Well, um, I was hoping that, ah, we could chat informally on these matters as one friend to another," Father Martin meekly replied.

"The minute that I became aware that this conversation would focus on your current work assignment, you forced my hand to treat this as official business of the Church. I had no recourse but to call the Bishop and tell him that we were meeting today; he is expecting my call right after we talk. Now tell me exactly what the heck you got yourself into so that I can help you work out of this mess."

Father Martin slid down in his chair, rubbing his fingers on his forehead, feeling like a grade school student sitting in front of the principle, trying to explain his actions in order to avoid Saturday detention. The somber mood in the room did nothing to alleviate this present feeling. Father Martin took Father Paul through all that he knew about James Montgomery and what little he knew of Dr. Junger, and then tried to justify why he thought it was important to move faster than the snail's pace that most investigations moved at before approval was given on a certain course of action.

"Father Martin, did it ever occur to you that, by fully informing the Bishop or I where James Montgomery and his family were flying off to, we could've had the sense and foresight to stop him? We could have kept him and his family in the States until we had time to sort this out and rationally figure out the next move; we have enough clout for that in the United States, but you never gave us the chance to act at all. From what you told me, James Montgomery and his family are out of the country by now, heading into territories in Asia where we have less influence. You have actually reduced the number of options that the Church has in dealing with this situation. How many times have I told you in the past, suppress the emotions, think, plan, and then react? You lost all logic in this situation — why?"

"I just thought it would take weeks to explain to the Bishop what I thought should be done, and by that time it would be too late."

"Hold on, Father Martin. When you were summarizing this for me, you yourself said that you didn't want James to leave the country, and that you wanted to talk to Dr. Junger right away. Is that the extent of your grand plan?"

"Well, when you put it that way, the logic sounds rather trite, but at the time, I..."

Father Paul interrupted him in mid-sentence. "So, at the time, you already concluded that nothing could be done to prevent James Montgomery from leaving the country, and you wanted to do the next best thing as soon as possible to appease your sense of urgency; is that correct?"

The stare from Father Martin provided the answer.

"Father Martin, I must say for all that you have accomplished; sometimes I think that you haven't learned anything at all. What is it about James Montgomery that caused you to overreact?"

"Well, he is very unique. He has a family now, and we've gotten close."

"You got close to him, and he has a family now. Remember that he has no soul—you have no moral obligation to save him, and he has killed many people who also have families. What do you have to say about that?"

Father Martin reared up in his chair. "I'm going to tell you this: from all the conversations that I had with this being, I know that he is special and that God has allowed him to exist and be put on this earth for a reason, which I believe will ultimately serve Him."

"Oh, and should we overlook that he is a common murderer that has no remorse and cannot show any acts of contrition?"

"So the Church wants to intercede on its own interests without fully understanding the situation? Sounds just like the Inquisition to me," Father Martin replied acerbically, without thinking.

"I am going to ignore that childish remark," said Father Paul in a stern voice. "Might I suggest that you reflect on your vows to the Church and God while you are here?"

"Well, this conversation has gone to hell in a handbag. I am sorry for my smart aleck remarks, but I am going to reiterate something here and for the record if you like. James Montgomery is part of something that is not man-made; he is special and fits into God's plan somehow, and all my intuition tells me that. You can continue to logically tear apart my reasoning now because I don't have all the facts necessary to argue with you. But I will tell you and the Bishop this: I am going to get the facts."

"Now, this is the Father Martin that I have been waiting to hear from; I was wondering if he was still in there. So, when do you meet with Dr. Junger?"

"I have a meeting with him at 4 PM today at the Clinic."

"Have you formulated a plan on what you are going to ask him?"

"Not exactly. I was hoping to get into that a little bit with you today, but we don't have much time left before I need to leave."

Giving a big sigh, Father Paul said, "Well, you better go through with the meeting, and then we can chat afterwards and *think* through what should be done next after your conversation with him. In the meantime, I will inform the Bishop of the James Montgomery situation and your meeting with Dr. Junger."

Father Martin stood up and shook hands with Father Paul. "Thank you. You have always been there for me, even though I don't always like the message that is delivered."

"Good luck, and don't forget to call me later. You pinned a Bishop on my back; you owe me one for that."

Father Martin walked out of the office; the conversation hadn't gone as he expected, but the stern lecture had set him back on course. He would have to decide how to confront Dr. Junger on the James Montgomery situation as he drove up to Chadds Ford.

When Father Paul was sure that Father Martin had left, he called the Bishop and informed him of the conversation. The Bishop was not pleased with the events as they transpired to date.

"Father Paul, I told you that I wanted him chastised, remorseful, and heading back to Florida with his tail between his legs today!"

"That wasn't possible—I couldn't pull it off. He has the sense that something big is going on here, and he is determined to see it through."

"I don't like him meeting with Dr. Junger alone; if he finds out or suspects in any way that Junger is assisting us in this matter, then things could get difficult. Frankly, I don't trust Junger at all; he may tell Father Martin everything just for the fun of it. And right now, I can't trust Father Martin to toe the line."

"Understood. Let's see what transpires after their talk; I will call you as soon as I know anything."

"Alright," replied the Bishop. "And don't worry about how late it is when you call; I'm not going to be able to get any sleep until I know what Father Martin has learned, and what he plans to do next. Are you sure that you can still read him?"

"Like a book, sir; like a book."

Father Martin turned off I-95 at the Wilmington Delaware exit that lead to Route 202. As he drove past Independence Mall and approached Fairfax Shopping Center, a flood of pleasant memories overcame him, as he remembered sharing leisure Saturdays with his middle school friends in autumn. The weather was usually crisp and overcast: perfect for sweatshirts, jeans, and playing rag-tag games of touch football. On more adventurous days, when they had some money, they would catch the early afternoon bus that ran along 202 and take it up to Concord High School. They weren't really interested in watching the high school football game that was going on at the time—the Concord High School cheerleaders were enough to capture their imaginations. Now they were always something to ogle over. After making a few loops around the perimeter of the football field, they would walk over to the Concord Mall and grab a bite to eat while enjoying several more discrete, yet flirtatious, rounds of girl-watching with girls their own age. When they lost interest with that, they would trek several miles to the Fairfax Shopping Center

Bowling Alley, where they would spend the rest of the day bowling, playing pool and pinball.

He remembered how joyous it was to be young. Your time was occupied with school, homework, the required home chores and family outings, endless thoughts of what girl might be interested in you, and what you were going to do with your friends to fight boredom the rest of the time. Father Martin wished that he could return to those times; he suspected that many people often felt the same way when stress from work, family matters, or personal problems overwhelmed them, making them question every major decision that they made in their lives. At times like this, he became his own worst critic, and he wondered if his judgment was still good enough, if he could still be objective and rational. He also wondered why he became so belligerent on certain issues, and if his older age was starting to bias his actions. Most of all, he wondered if his decision to dedicate his life to God was based on a true calling, or was he simply taking an easier road in life. Reflecting on this for a moment, he concluded that marriage, children, cook-outs, and suburban life would have left him unfulfilled; he yearned to help a broader base of people than just his immediate family, and to a large extent he had done just that until he took on this new role for the Church some seventeen years ago. This job is what had taken him off-course from his calling. When he first became a priest, the job was extremely fulfilling and energizing. For over a decade, he was helping people and organizations everywhere; for a time, he never knew what part of the world he was going to. However, as the years passed, he began handling sensitive ecclesiastical matters until these assignments became his sole responsibility. Before he met James, he was beginning to doubt if he would ever get back to helping anyone directly.

Looking up at the stop light ahead, Father Martin realized that he was approaching Route 1; the Clinic was just a few minutes away in Chadds Ford, and he hadn't given an ounce of thought to how he was going to handle the dialogue with

Dr. Junger. He couldn't even remember the last time that he had been this ill-prepared. This was one of the most important meetings that he was going to have in his life, and he was just going to wing it.

Visibly stressed, he began to breathe harder; his chest cramped up a bit, and he realized that he was starting to have an anxiety attack. Letting up on the gas, he slowed the car down, pulled off to the side of the road, and rolled down the window to let some fresh air in. Taking a few deep breaths seemed to calm him down. Still pensive, but under control, he reached the gates to the Preston Estates at 3:52 PM, just as he finished saying a quartet of short prayers, two of which he had written himself in Seminary School.

SuiLeng started to speak, but then she just stopped and gawked at James. SuiLeng speechless, if even for a second, might have been a comical moment, but with her forehead striated with worry lines and her eyebrows almost knitted together, the look of concern and confusion that James saw on her face made him feel awful. He felt that she was beginning to comprehend that they might not be prepared to deal with all the dynamics at work here. As SuiLeng glanced at her boys then back at James again, he could nearly read her mind.

"We did the right thing leaving Florida; no one in the States can help us at this point in time. In Asia, we have your family; they will help us."

"James, your past is so convoluted. Here I thought that we were dealing with something current, of this time, something that both of us could see. Now, I have no idea what part of your life is chasing us, and what set of circumstances in your life to review for clues as to what might happen in the near future."

"We'll be all right. I know what I have to do to protect our family."

"What makes you so sure that we are handling this right? How do you know that we aren't just putting more of my family at risk?"

"SuiLeng, this much is clear: I have to get you and the boys someplace safe. In order to chart our next set of actions, I have to become mentally and physically much stronger than I am now. The only place that we can accomplish both things is in Penang."

"Why Penang? We have lots of money, more than enough to live on for years; why can't we find some other place in the world to hide and think about a way to resolve this? Why do we have to risk more of my family with our troubles?"

Seeing that SuiLeng was coming unglued, he needed to walk her through the next few minutes gently. "SuiLeng, your family loves you, PB and CS with all their hearts. They would be extremely insulted and hurt if I didn't call and ask them for help; your grandmother even said that she would have put a curse on me for lifetimes to come if I kept arguing about involving them in this matter and didn't get you and the boys over there immediately. Sounds just like your grandmother, doesn't it?"

James noted that SuiLeng smiled when he mentioned her grandmother. She and her grandmother had a special relationship; the tough, intelligent, and mischievous nature that SuiLeng displayed surely came from her.

"Your brother, on the other hand, wasn't as nice as your grandmother; to paraphrase him, if anything happened to you or the boys before I got there, then he would dedicate his entire life to make my life a living hell until he figured out some way to kill me."

"Humph, that sounds just like Winston. You know he is worse than one of those moray eels — he not only bites and never lets go when he wants to hurt you, but he also keeps kicking you just to let you know that he is still mad. Okay, I can accept that my family wants to help, but do they really understand the danger that we are bringing them?"

"SuiLeng, where did you think you got your skills to see people's auras from?"

"From my grandmother, of course." Puzzled, SuiLeng asked why he asked her that question, but she got another question from him instead.

"And do you think your brother possesses any of these skills?"

"Well, I suppose so." Just then, the light bulb clicked on in SuiLeng's mind.

"So you are saying that my grandmother and brother knew the essence of what you were and the implications of your life long before I did, and they decided a long time ago that they were okay with that?" SuiLeng paused for a second. "Otherwise they would never have allowed you to be part of my life."

"Correct," replied James.

"So how much more do they know about your life than I do?" SuiLeng's voice was full of suspicion.

Sensing the trap about to be set, James answered cautiously. "Your grandmother knows a lot more than you do, but your brother only knows a bit more."

"And why does he know more than your wife knows?"

"Because the trust built up by working with him previously allowed me to disclose other information about myself, now that I need to evolve."

Father Martin informed the guard at the gate that he had a 4 PM appointment with Dr. Junger. The frown on the security guard's face didn't help to settle his nerves.

"May I see a driver's license and another form of ID, Father?"

"Of course," replied Father Martin. Fumbling with his wallet, he pulled out his driver's license and social security card and handed them to the guard.

"Okay, I am going to have to ask you to pull over into that parking lot while I sort this out."

Looking at the parking lot fifty yards away, Father Martin asked why he couldn't wait right here. Surely it would only take a second to confirm his appointment.

The security guard answered gruffly, "I would do that Father, but since you aren't on the appointment sheet, and they are updated and verified throughout the day; I am going to have to ask you to pull into that parking lot over there before I make a call to confirm anything—that is our procedure."

Seeing that he wasn't going to make any headway unless he complied, Father Martin reluctantly pulled into the parking lot, turned off the ignition and got out of his car.

Impervious to Father Martin's frustration, the security guard stood where he was and watched him the entire time before he slowly walked back to his partners at the gatehouse. Father Martin leaned against the driver side door and glared at the security guards in the booth.

A shift change occurred in the security booth at 4 PM sharp; this took 15 minutes to complete, since cars coming both in and out were required to go through security checks. Finally, at 4:20 PM, a different guard motioned for Father Martin to drive to the gate. He had to show his driver's license again, which this guard took to the gatehouse to have it scanned in. He was then asked if he would comply with a second security check, which was an inspection of his car. If so, then he had to sign and date two forms of consent for the inspection. If he refused, then he could not enter the facility.

It took 15 more minutes for the second security check to be completed; they looked inside the car, the glove compartment, the trunk, and the engine block. They also scanned the undercarriage of the car with mirrors. At one point, Father Martin had to laugh out loud at the incredulous behavior that he was witnessing; he wasn't going through customs into a new country, he was just trying to have a meeting. He kept wondering to himself what the heck they were looking for. Finally, he received a parking number assignment and a temporary security badge that only allowed him to enter the Clinic's main doors.

At 4:50 PM, he approached the doors to the Clinic. However, inside the building, things were just as ludicrous. He was required to read and sign a confidentiality agreement and to submit to a pat down in a side room, where his tape recorder was taken away from him. Still upset by the pat down, he bluntly asked why they just couldn't have told him that no tape recorders were allowed. The reply to his question was a short answer stating that he could pick up his tape recorder later at the main security desk after his meeting. Disheveled and annoyed, at 5:20 PM, Father Martin was escorted to Dr. Junger's office.

Since neither Dr. Junger nor Father Martin had ever seen one another before, both of them absorbed the other's presence as they shook hands. Like all people who meet Dr. Junger for the first time, Father Martin felt inadequate compared to the handsome, physical prowess that the other man possessed. But what was most intimidating was seeing the intelligence move within Dr. Junger's eyes; Father Martin would never be able to match wits with this man even if he had prepared a year for this meeting.

Dr. Junger noted Father Martin's broad shoulders and firm handshake, but saw a little pouch around his belly, which conveyed he did not exercise regularly. The dark spots under his brown eyes, along with a full head of gray hair, also suggested that Father Martin either suffered from insomnia or had a job that kept him from getting enough sleep.

With a little hint of mockery in his voice, Dr. Junger started the conversation.

"Father Martin, good to meet you. I see that you made it through security mostly unscathed."

Irritated and having his Irish temper kick in, Father Martin was ready to bark a little before engaging in a civil conversation. "I thought that we had a 4 PM appointment? And if I may ask, just what is it exactly that you are trying to accomplish with your security checks?"

"Isn't it obvious, Father? We are trying to protect the material and physical assets at this complex by keeping all harmful and undesirable elements from getting in and stealing it. Top notch biomedical and industrial research is conducted on this site. A breach in security would greatly undermine the brand name that this prestigious facility has earned over the years."

"If by physical assets, you mean people, then hasn't two suicide attempts created a blemish on the brand name?"

Laughing out loud, Dr. Junger replied, "Excellent epee thrust, excellent. Perhaps talking with you won't be a total waste of my time after all." Pausing for effect and to ensure that the last remark sunk in, Dr. Junger continued. "You know, I've been in meetings all day; would you mind walking around the grounds and chatting? They are quite beautiful this time of year."

Having recovered some dignity in the short exchange of words to this point, Father Martin also agreed that it would be a good idea to walk around the grounds and chat.

Exiting the building and walking in the opposite direction from the route that John Parella, Jr. took on the day that he decided to leave the Clinic by way of its east wall, Dr. Junger and Father Martin strolled along the path that bordered the back wall of the estate. All the annuals had been planted and were in full bloom; the lawn had a manicured look better than the finest golf course that Father Martin had ever been on, and, while the afternoon sun still made the air hot and muggy in places, a slight breeze and the shade from ample maple trees along the path created an agreeable ambiance for a meeting.

Dr. Junger noticed that Father Martin was taking in the landscaping and the architectural grandeur that made this modern facility feel like an eighteenth century early American town.

Commenting on his observation, Dr. Junger said, "You know the design of this complex, along with its paths and gardens and the selection of all building material are exact representations of the lifestyle that wealthy, early Americans enjoyed in the Northeast at that time."

Father Martin looked away as if talking to some distant stranger as he answered. "An interesting choice of words, Dr. Junger, with both implied meaning to the past and to the present conversation that we are about to have. So wealth builds countries and enjoys the fruits of its labor. But for wealth to enjoy such privilege there must be less fortunate individuals to take advantage of; otherwise, wealth would have no leverage at all."

"Well, if I didn't know better, then I would have said at first blush that you were an enlightened, lambent individual, but the truth is that you are just as hypocritical as the rest of the well-educated wealthy individuals are in this country. You purport to be a champion of the poor and down trodden, but the truth is, Father, that you have never felt their pain; you lead a privileged life yourself, enjoying all the benefits that an upper middle class family can provide. And even now, as an adult, you never have to worry about losing your job, or wondering where your next meal will comes from; the Church will provide that for you the rest of your life. And in the last seventeen years, the philanthropic lifestyle that you lead as a priest, a lifestyle that validated your calling to God, has been replaced by parlous missions for the Church."

Seeing the surprised expression on Father Martin's face, Dr. Junger continued. "Father, I make it a point to learn all that I can about the people that I have to interact with or deal with. I don't need to trust someone to work with them; all I need to know is whether they are trustworthy or not, and if they have values or not, and then I know how to work with them and through them on all matters that concern us. So, how would you label yourself? Be truthful now; I can usually tell by a person's voice if they are stretching the truth or not."

Shocked at the terse remarks, but still focused, Father Martin responded, "What type of person I am is irrelevant to the matter that I have come to inquire about. More germane to my interest is what type of person you are, and to what extent you plan on continuing to manipulate people's lives, first by allowing two suicide attempts to occur on these grounds, and second by inciting James Montgomery to flee this country."

Dr. Junger stopped walking. He looked perplexed for an instant, and Father Martin suspected that for the first time in a long time, someone finally had enough verve to confront the infamous, egotistical Dr. Junger and declare him a maniacal person.

Holding his hands on his hips, Dr. Junger laughed even louder than in his office. It was unnerving to Father Martin; he had no clue what he had said that made Dr. Junger so jocular.

"Can it be? Can it really be that you have come here to talk to me without the Church's permission—without the Bishop approving your visit? Such impious behavior, such gall, and since I know that you are not a fool, that would tell me that you are still a man with personal conviction. Well, you have answered my question: I can trust you, at least for now. Given enough time, it may even turn out that I grow fond of you and your exploits."

Father Martin's demeanor conveyed that he had been found out; he really was there without the Bishop's permission. Putting his hands behind his back and resuming their walk with a light bounce in his step, Dr. Junger opened up. "So, Father Martin, what is it that you would like to know?"

Chapter 20

REVELATIONS FROM DR. JUNGER

For a second or two, Father Martin was dumbfounded. Had he heard Dr. Junger correctly? Did the man just give him permission to ask any questions that he wanted? Here, Father Martin had thought that he was somehow going to have to bully or bluff Dr. Junger into a dialogue through the suggestion that the Church was displeased with his activities and ulterior motives. Yet it was he who became intimidated by the security checks at the Clinic and by the physical and intellectual prowess of Dr. Junger. In reality, his brazen visit had earned him a modicum of trust, which implied several things: that Dr. Junger was not intimidated by the power base of the Church, or that he was somehow working within boundary conditions that were acceptable to the Church, at the moment. These revelations created a whole new set of questions.

Coaxing Father Martin, Dr. Junger spoke first. "Well, Father, should we just stroll along and enjoy the afternoon sun, or should we stop at the bench ahead and chat?"

Back from his private thoughts, Father Martin glanced at the rustic bench ahead and the shade provided from surrounding trees. "I've been driving so much lately that a stroll to stretch the legs sounded good at first, but the harried pace of the last few days has caught up to me—let's sit and talk."

Before both men were settled into the oak planks on the bench, questions emanated from Father Martin.

"Dr. Junger, how did you surmise that I was here of my own volition?"

"Oh c'mon, that should be obvious."

"So, you've talked with the Bishop on matters concerning James Montgomery?"

"Not just talked, but also advised. James is a unique individual, wouldn't you agree? Explaining his presence on earth is difficult enough; explaining that his presence on earth might be a good thing took a lot of convincing. I was the one that suggested that the angelic pair of priests and you visit James at his house to confirm his nature."

Astounded, Father Martin turned and stared at Dr. Junger. "You suggested that to the Bishop? Oh, that explains a lot. It was such a brilliant idea; it ended all the internal squabbling. I was so pleased with the Bishop. Privately, I actually drew parallels between the Bishop and King Solomon on how he handled that matter. Well, I should have known better."

"Now, now, Father, I thought that men in your position were not supposed to pre-judge any person—that's God's domain, isn't it? Besides, you have to at least credit the Bishop for listening to the idea and acting on it."

Nodding his head in agreement, Father Martin continued his questions. "So, how long have you been advising the Church in this matter and in other matters?"

"Those topics are off limits. If your superiors had wanted you to know that, you would have been told by now. It's not my place to enlighten you in those areas. Why don't we talk about James himself—isn't he the real reason that you came all this way?"

Gemini Ascending

"Alright, but you did acknowledge that you were advising the Church in this matter; so, you must know that I will press my superiors on why I wasn't told of your involvement previously, which will create a great deal of havoc in its own right." The raised eyebrows and twinkle in Dr. Junger's eyes conveyed that he was counting on Father Martin to create a stink on why he was left out of the loop.

"So, Dr. Junger, just what is James, and why do you believe he is here at this moment in time?"

"It's really no fun answering that question outright; let's start by what you know. James is a being without a soul that possesses incredible strength, and, as you have reported to your superiors, he can continue to evolve. You have already assessed his present state of existence and found him to be relatively harmless to mankind at the moment even though he has a propensity for dispensing Old Testament justice when it comes to people who prey on weaker individuals. Given these facts Father, along with your extensive study of the Bible, what do you think James could be?"

"Hmmm, the Book of Numbers references the Anakim, who were a race of giants that made the Israelites look like grasshoppers, but my research on them suggests an over exaggeration of their size and capabilities. On the other hand, the Book of Genesis refers to the enigmatic Nephilim, who were born of the sons of Heaven and daughters of Earth, and went on to be heroes of old, men of renown."

"Yes, anyone can read those verses and speculate, but you've gotten special permission to study the Vatican archives three times over the years; what have those inquiries revealed to you?"

Stunned, Father Martin stuttered on his next question. "How could you possibly know that?"

With a slightly irritated tone, Dr. Junger replied, "What I know and how I have acquired certain information over the years is not the centerpiece of this discussion. So, I will ask you one more time: what did you learn, or better yet what hypothesis did you formulate, and then answer, from your studies?"

"Well, I have concluded that stories sung by bards and written accounts of events always have an element of truth to them, and that to find the unadulterated truth, one has to meticulously uncover and peel away the storyteller's personal biases. In the case of the Nephilim, I actually concluded that they existed and that they formed the basis for the Greek Gods."

"Very good, Father. Now what if I told you that James was, until now, thought to be a mythological creature, and that he has a fraternal brother?"

"Mythological creature I would believe. But you're also telling me that he has a brother! Where does his brother live; why hasn't James ever mentioned him before; does the Bishop know about any of this?"

"Well that got you going. Actually, James can't tell you much about his brother because he doesn't know anything about him yet. They sensed each other in the womb as they grew, but the only glimpse that they had of one another was during birth as they were sent to their respective destinies. It is very rare that the males of his kind are sent to the same place or coexist in the same time; they usually end up well apart from one another at first. That was the case with James and his brother. And no, the Church does not know that James has a brother. They haven't connected the dots to realize that the males of James' race are always born as fraternal twins. They would be quite distraught to find that out; therefore, I have decided to keep that information to myself. You will have to make up your own mind if and when you ever divulge this."

"How do you know all this?"

"James told me himself. I spent a few months with him a long time ago. It was the one point in his life when he was in such a state of physical duress and pain that he actually thought he would die. Would you like to hear the story?"

"Yes," was all Father Martin could say.

"James and his little entourage were raucously exiting a Tokyo bar late one evening. The streets were poorly lit, but I could see that he was literally carrying one woman on his left arm, one on his right arm, while he had a third woman's arms draped around his neck. They were all conversing in Japanese, and, at first blush, they were having one heck of time. I believe that James had every intention of bedding all three of them; he was energetic enough for that in those days, but it turned out that he was just being set up to be robbed."

"After crossing through a few alleys, James ran into three men with swords — men who knew how to use them. The women ran away after James set them down; unfortunately, the men weren't just after James' money; they wanted to hurt him. Alcohol never had much effect on James' reflexes, but these men were highly skilled and fast. James disabled one of them outright, but the other two sliced off his left hand, took three fingers and knuckles off his right hand, slashed both his legs, and slit his throat wide open. After taking his money pouch, they spit on him, kicked him several times, and walked away."

"I sensed that James might not be human when I first saw him walk out of the bar, but the fear and vulnerability in his pleading eyes, when I approached, created some doubt about my initial assessment. Observing him for several seconds to see what he would do, he soon realized that I was just watching him, triggering momentary anger that snapped him back to his natural instincts. Glaring at me, he ripped off a section of his shirt with his two remaining fingers and pressed it around his throat to stop the bleeding. Beings like James can coagulate blood and heal arteries or veins on any part of their body with mild pressure. He was attempting to do the same with his legs when I reached down to assist him."

"My god, Doctor, why didn't you help him right away?"

"I wanted to be sure that he was what I thought he was, and I wanted to see how he handled the situation."

"Are you kidding me? That's barbaric," replied Father Martin.

"Not at all Father, you learn the most by seeing how living organisms respond during periods of intense duress. Would you like me to continue, or do you want to debate the humanity of my decisions at the time?"

"Continue."

"I walked miles with James that night. We needed to go deep into the district that we were in to purchase the kind of medical help that he required, the kind of discrete help that I trusted. With my night coat draped around his shoulders, I washed the blood off of him at a public fountain. It was a surreal experience, trudging through a moonless night with an immortal without speaking a single word. He only needed to lean into me slightly to keep his balance, but other than that he managed to walk the entire distance on his own. I was impressed, and, as you can imagine, I am not a person who is easily impressed."

"When I had James situated in a safe place, he clutched a quill pen, that I had in the room, with the two fingers he had left and wrote down what assistance he would need to heal faster. While his body had the ability to heal naturally, medical assistance dramatically reduces his recovery time. It took a few operations, under my supervision, to realign his throat and leg muscles, but he wouldn't let anyone touch his hands. Feeding him while also washing his wounds and hands each day for nine weeks, I witnessed an amazing regenerative process that human ancestors had lost a long time ago. He was able to talk a little in the third week; by the fifth week, we were able to converse freely."

"What did you talk about during the last four weeks?"

"When I told James that I was a doctor and the type of patients that I dealt with, we spent nearly all the time discussing the hundreds of years that he had lived, the knowledge that he was born with, and the ultimate purpose of his life."

"And what is the purpose of his life, Dr. Junger?"

"James and his kind serve three basic purposes: they guard worlds, they build worlds, or they rule worlds. Even the devil is scared of what this race is capable of doing."

"So you are talking about the Apocalypse?"

"Oh, for goodness sake Father, stay with me, and please get the mud out of your thought processes. Why is it that every cleric who hears a sentence with the words 'rule worlds' or the word 'devil' in it automatically jumps to the conclusion that the end of the world is coming. The earth might have reached its half-life, but it will survive for another one to five billion years before the sun burns out in this solar system."

"Who are you?"

"I like to think of myself as a facilitator, a being who has general power of attorney so to speak."

"Dr. Junger, you actually have the arrogance to sit there and tell me that you are acting in the best interests of the people of this world and in the best interest of James?"

"No, I didn't say that; the conditions for my decisions are not decided by the people of this world, especially beings who have the petulance to continually question the Creator's existence and His rules."

"But we were given free will; our fate is decided by what we do individually."

"That is true for the individual soul, but the fate of worlds is decided by what the aggregate population does. This world's constant foray into eugenics, its declining moral structure, its contentious behavior between and within religions, its propensity for continuous ethnic cleansing, and its irritating attitude of science for science sake will be its undoing. Remember, this is the Creator who brought the flood, and the flood story is really a metaphor for the destruction of the majority of mortal life on Earth."

"What? Wait a minute, now I'm really confused. I thought that you said a little while ago that the earth has at least a billion years left, and that we were not talking about the Apocalypse."

"That's correct, Father. Remember, some people actually survived the Flood, and, while He was a little distraught over that decision, if push comes to shove, an artist has no choice but to re-paint the portions of the canvas that He deems as unworthy. "

Standing up and pointing his forefinger at Dr. Junger, Father Martin lashed out in anger. "You actually want me to believe that you coordinate with the Creator? That you have a power lunch with the Boss every now and then in order to give Him an update on how things are going? You have the mendacity of a used car salesmen. I think I'm done here Dr. Junger; this is the biggest bunch of crap that I have ever heard in my life."

"I don't care what you believe. You're the one who stuck your nose into this; so, you might as well hear what I have to say and then decide for yourself what your parochial education will allow you to consider as truth. Now, sit down!"

Mumbling to himself, Father Martin grudgingly sat down again.

"Thank you, Father. Now if we go back to the Nephilim, I will recite some of the verses that were left out of the Bible.

"The Lord God granted the gift of Life to all women of the world, and to all creatures of the world for this gift was good. He also granted the gift of Life and Creation to all men of the world and to the Sons of Heaven. The physical union of men and women produced children who toiled on the earth and fastened goodness from it, and the Lord God was pleased. The Sons of Heaven and the daughters of Earth created children who had the strength and power to tame the world and fasten lasting goodness from their works, and the Lord God was pleased with this. The children of Sons of Heaven and the daughters of Earth built great cities in the ocean lands, in fertile land, and in the mountains; these children created vessels to sail the Heavens and guide others to this world, and the Lord God was pleased. These children worshipped and gave praise to the Lord God for their existence, and this was good, and the Lord God was pleased."

"But the Sons of Heaven became jealous over praise given to the Lord God for the creation of their children. The Sons of Heaven demanded sacrifices, gifts and praise for the powers bestowed upon their children. When the Lord God saw this, He became angry that

false gods were being worshipped. The Lord God demanded the Sons of Heaven and their children to worship only Him. When they would not listen to the word of the Lord, the first battle of heaven was fought, and many Sons of Heaven were cast out; their power to create was taken away from them, and they were locked away for all eternity. Their children, who did not worship the Lord God, also suffered the same fate, and their great works were destroyed by the Lord God."

"Are you saying that Atlantis and some of the ancient, deserted cities in Mesoamerica, the Middle East and Asia were built from the children of the Sons of Heaven?"

"Yes, Father, they literally assisted in the mounds, pyramid structures, cities, and the astronomical markings around the world."

"Did any of the children of the Sons of Heaven survive imprisonment?"

"Excellent question. Some of them were spared for their belief and worship in the Lord God, but there is one question that I am surprised you haven't asked yet, Father."

"What's that?"

"What guards the gates, worlds and dimensions that hold the cast out Sons of Heaven and their children from re-entering Heaven, this world, or the Universe?"

"I think I know," declared Father Martin. "It would have to be a race so powerful, so fierce, that it could control all of them. And for this race to still fear the power of the Creator, they would have to be born without souls; so, if they were to disobey the Creator, their fate would be the end of their existence."

"Correct, Father, you now have half the story; ready for the rest?"

"That's a rhetorical question, right?"

"Yes, but let me ask one that isn't rhetorical. Why would the Creator free the Israelites from Egyptian slavery, give them strict instruction not to kill one another, yet allow them to kill men and women that lived in the Promised Land while they conquered it?"

"I don't know; I have never been able to reconcile this. Either we have a cruel and jealous God that we worship, or the story of the siege of the Land of Canaan is an extreme rationalization, in the name of God, for taking over someone else's property: kind of like the Crusades in the Middle Ages."

"Father, remember your earlier statements about peeling away the biases to find the truth. Today, the Old Testament is viewed as an anachronism to the teachings of the New Testament. But what if the remaining children of the Sons of Heaven ruled portions of the earth, and some of their children and grandchildren lost their way and became false gods for their subjects to praise and worship? As an initial solution to this problem, the Creator freed the Israelites and promised them the Land of Milk and Honey if they would purge the unbelievers from this land. But what being among the Israelites was strong enough to defeat the children and grandchildren of the Sons of Heaven, and merciless enough to kill them if they fought or resisted capture?"

In a low voice, Father Martin answered, "A being that had no soul, a being like James."

"Yes, but not just a being like James. It was his brother, along with others like him that the Lord God sent to Earth. These beings have the power to see inside others; they can see one's essence or soul, and they know with certainty, as God does, if another being is false or not. And they killed with such atrocity that the Creator, through Moses, decreed that everyone who touched a dead body had to cleanse or purify themselves over a seven day period."

With his forehead sweating and throat choked with emotion, Father Martin squeaked out a question that was barely audible. "Is this James' purpose in life also?"

"As he evolves, this could be his destiny. As I said, James and his kind will either help this world and the other forty vital celestial planets in the Universe, or he and his brother and their race will eventually conquer and rule all these worlds. And it would be extremely sad if the latter becomes the fate of this world and the Universe. The Creator, over time, has sent beautiful messages to the people of this world through his Prophets; all they had to do was faithfully follow those messages."

"Did you share any of this with my superiors?"

"Father, the Church has collected knowledge for nearly two thousand years, while only showing the world a thimble's worth of information. They know most of what I told you. They have always suspected what species killed the unbelievers thousands of years ago. They also have a good idea of what James is here to do; they just don't know that James' brother is intimately tied to this situation. Therefore, in order to give the world a fighting chance to decide its destiny, I decided at the turn of this century to share information with other faiths so that they would understand the magnitude of what was happening. This information was revealed to the sons of Ishmael in Saudi Arabia, who hand-picked people around the world to bear the burden of this knowledge with them and act upon it."

"Dr. Junger, you are much different than I expected. In essence, if what you say is true, then I can't figure out one thing: why does James mistrust you so much?"

"Well, how did you think James reacted when I told him that I was the one who arranged to have him attacked in Tokyo?"

Chapter 21

ANGER

Dr. Junger stared into a scarlet face, spittle spewing from Father Martin's mouth; a clenched fist was one half inch from his nose before the verbal tirade began.

"You self-righteous bastard! What gives you the right to conduct experiments on living beings? Do you derive some sadistic, lecherous satisfaction from these acts, or are you really just a perverted person wrapped in expensive clothing? I am sick of—"

Before he could finish the sentence, Dr. Junger grabbed a finger on his other hand. Intense pain radiated throughout Father Martin's body. It was as if every nerve ending in his body had been triggered by a high voltage charge; his breath seized in his lungs and each limb of his body began to shake. The muscle spasms in Father Martin became so severe that he was actually bouncing up and down a few inches off the ground. While still holding Father Martin's finger, Dr. Junger stood up, and used his finger as a steering wheel, slowly turning Father Martin around until his back faced the bench again. When he let go of his finger, Father Martin collapsed into the bench. The last sight that he saw was the smug smile on Dr. Junger's face.

Three minutes later, Father Martin regained consciousness. His head and body felt like a train had hit him. Taking deep breaths to clear his mind, he spoke slowly, as if suffering from a humungous hangover. "You didn't have to do that."

"On the contrary, you were working yourself up into quite a hysterical state; you left me little choice to quell the situation."

"So your actions are above reproach?"

"As I said Father, I am a facilitator, and only a select few in this Universe are capable of commenting on my actions."

"Oh, only a select few can comment on your behavior? Must be nice to have all that power. Is anyone allowed to criticize your actions and hold you accountable for them?"

"My goodness, you can be exhausting; perhaps it would be helpful to clear the fog from your mind before we continue." Reaching over, Dr. Junger pressed his thumb above the bridge of Father Martin's nose, in the space between his eyebrows. In two seconds, Father Martin felt refreshed, full of energy; all the aches in his body had evaporated, and it was as if he had awoken from the deepest, most relaxing night's sleep he ever had.

"Whoa, if the pharmaceutical industry knew you could do that, they would pay you millions to keep it a secret or give them the exclusive rights. Where did you get your power from?"

"Father, the power that I have now was given to me, and that is all that you need to know about me at the moment. My job, as a facilitator, is to ensure that this world and the Universe move in a certain direction; it is up to my discretion on how I accomplish this, and who I involve in this endeavor."

"Does the Bishop or Father Paul know who—or what—you really are?"

"Well, Father Martin, why don't you ask them when you see them again? I am sure that they will be very interested in our conversation."

"Yeah, I'm sure they will. Getting back to James, what purpose did it serve to tell him that you were the one who had him attacked?"

"Several actually, first, I didn't want James to hunt down

and kill the men who attacked him. However, James didn't see it that way, taking offense to being attacked, and being a bit immature about the whole thing. Second, I wanted to wake James up, make him realize that his existence in this world was not happenstance, make him realize that his life had purpose, and that there were many forces in the world that would want to shape the direction his life took, or eliminate him."

Getting agitated again, Father Martin responded, "Immature about the whole thing; what the hell does that mean? How would you expect someone to react when you slice them up? My god, you may be intelligent, but you surely lack common sense. I mean, really..."

"Am I going to have to zap you again, Father?"

"No, I'll be okay; I just can't believe what comes out of your mouth sometimes."

"What exactly is so hard to believe? In some areas, James has even more power than I do. What purpose would it serve him to hunt down and kill the men who attacked him, when they actually taught him a valuable lesson. James always knew that he could be hurt, and he knew that he could be killed; however, he never realized how quickly it could be done. I told James all this, and yet he still chose to exact revenge on these men. If James were a mob boss, then perhaps the logic of his actions would be clear. But besides me, only a few other people knew that these men attacked him."

"Then perhaps James was sending a message to you. Perhaps his message is to leave him alone."

"Yes, that would be the obvious conclusion, Father, except that I shared a great deal of information with him during the weeks that we were together. I told him what my purpose was, and how I operate; I even told him more about his brother, but in much greater detail than I shared with you. Therefore, given the value derived from the lessons that he learned, it just made no sense to kill indiscriminately like that."

"Oh, so killing with conviction is okay, is that it?"

"No, that's not what I do, if that is what you are implying. I am not allowed to directly intervene; I am only allowed to facilitate; therefore, I develop numerous plans based on events, putting many activities into motion with redundant players, if I am less certain about an outcome."

"So is that what I am, Dr. Junger, a redundant player?"

"That's up to you."

"What if I chose not to play?"

"Doesn't matter. Each player has choices, and I have to analyze all the choices that each player could make and then predict outcomes before they happen. I get surprised every now and then."

"You sure don't suffer from lack of self-confidence."

"I am darn good at what I do; it's why I continue to choose to do it. Can you make the same claim anymore?"

Father Martin paused a few seconds for self-reflection on the last seventeen years of his life before answering. "I am sure you know the answer to that already. When I first started out in the priesthood, I was able to help so many people. I had a keen insight into them—I could see their strife and their rationalizations, and I was always able to help them through their difficulties. This talent was rewarded with more challenging assignments over the years, but it took me further and further away from what I enjoyed doing the most, further away from my calling. My work was becoming one hundred percent secular in nature, and the spirituality that led me to the priesthood was ebbing away. I had just about resigned myself to this until I met James. He renewed the sense of purpose in me, representing the ultimate challenge that God could place before me: re-instilling values into a being without a soul."

"And you accuse *me* of having a big ego. Did it ever occur to you that you might not be up to the task of helping James, that his purpose in life is anathema to your renewed sense of purpose, that perhaps you're riding James' coattails the more that you learn about him?"

"I know that the relationship and trust which James and I

share is not coincidental. Our destinies are linked, and I don't have to hope that it is so; I know that it is so."

"Excellent Father, I would also concur with your assessment, especially after testing you the last few weeks to see if you had the conviction to show up here and meet with me."

"What's next, Dr. Junger?"

"We finish our conversation, and then you decide what you want to do."

"What you mean to say is that I will decide to do what you expect me to do, right?"

Chuckling lightly to himself, Dr. Junger did not reply.

WATCH FOR BOOK 2 IN THE
"GEMINI ASCENDING" SERIES
-later in 2018-

ACKNOWLEDGEMENTS

First, I would like to thank my family for providing continuous encouragement and feedback while patiently waiting for me to finish the initial book in this series.

I also want to thank all the people at Outskirts Press Inc., for their efforts and teamwork in the publishing process.

Lastly, I wholeheartedly would like to thank Paige Pfeifer for her diligence with the editing services that she provided.

BIBLIOGRAPHY

1. Arabian American Oil Company, "Arabic Work Vocabulary for Americans in Saudi Arabia" (Elias' Modern Press, Faggala, Cairo Second Edition 1946), page 33
2. Arabian American Oil Company, "Arabic Work Vocabulary for Americans in Saudi Arabia", page 33
3. Information from John M. Terranova conveyed to Mark J. Terranova
4. Arabian American Oil Company, "Arabic Work Vocabulary for Americans in Saudi Arabia", page 20
5. Arabian American Oil Company, "Arabic Work Vocabulary for Americans in Saudi Arabia", page 20
6. Arabian American Oil Company, "Arabic Work Vocabulary for Americans in Saudi Arabia", page 42
7. General Motor LocoMotives, "Wheels and Axles of Diesel Locomotives", (Electro Motive Division, La Grange, IL, circa 1950's), pages 4-23
8. John M. Terranova pictures shown to Mark J. Terranova
9. World Petroleum, "ARAMCO Field Operations" (World Petroleum, March 1953), pages 2-6.

10. World Petroleum, "ARAMCO Field Operations", pages 2-6
11. John M. Terranova pictures shown to Mark J. Terranova
12. General Motor LocoMotives, "Wheels and Axles of Diesel Locomotives", (Electro-Motive Division, La Grange, IL, circa 1950's), pages 4-23
13. Arabian American Oil Company, "Arabic Work Vocabulary for Americans in Saudi Arabia", pages 4 to 51
14. Arabian American Oil Company, "Arabic Work Vocabulary for Americans in Saudi Arabia", pages 4 to 51
15. John M. Terranova sharing knowledge with Mark J. Terranova
16. John M. Terranova pictures shown to Mark J. Terranova
17. Wikipedia, "Hajj", http://en.wikipedia.org/wiki/Hajj
18. Professor Sean Carroll, "Dark Matter, Dark Energy: The Dark Side of the Universe" (The Great Courses, 2007), pages 4-92 and Professor Sean Carroll, "Mysteries of Modern Physics: Time", (The Great Courses, 2007), pages 8-84
19. Professor Sean Carroll, "Dark Matter, Dark Energy: The Dark Side of the Universe", pages 4-92, and Professor Sean Carroll, "Mysteries of Modern Physics: Time", pages 8-84
20. Professor Sean Carroll, "Dark Matter, Dark Energy: The Dark Side of the Universe", pages 4-92, and Professor Sean Carroll, "Mysteries of Modern Physics: Time", pages 8-84
21. Professor Sean Carroll, "Dark Matter, Dark Energy: The Dark Side of the Universe", pages 4-92, and Professor Sean Carroll, "Mysteries of Modern Physics: Time", pages 8-84
22. "Chevreul Pendulum", www.shoners3.co.uk/pendulum.html

SPECIAL SECTION OF PICTURES FROM SAUDI ARABIA
-circa 1953 TO 1958-

ARABIC
WORK VOCABULARY
FOR AMERICANS
IN SAUDI ARABIA

PREPARED BY
EDUCATION DIVISION
PERSONNEL DEPARTMENT
ARABIAN AMERICAN OIL COMPANY
SAUDI ARABIA
1945
SECOND EDITION, REVISED
1946

Printed by : –
Elias' Modern Press, Faggala, Cairo.

— 33 —

Never put "al" at the beginning as well. *

If the first noun is a feminine ending in '-ah', this 'h' becomes a 't':

an oil company   sharikat zait
the window of the room   dariishat al Hijrah

A modifying adjective stands outside such a construction:

| the empty money-bag | kiis al fuluus al khaali |
| the big oil company | sharikat az zait al kabiirah |

---

* A common alternate method of tying nouns together is by use of the word "maal" (or "Hagg"). In this event "al" may be used without restrictions:

(al) kiis maal fuluus } (the) money-bag
(al) kiis Hagg fuluus }

With feminines a linking feminine ending is sometimes attached to the particle: minshaarah maalat Hadiid (for minshaarat Hadiid) (a hacksaw, lit., an "iron saw").

I always found it interesting that in this text (ARABIC Work Vocabulary for Americans in Saudi Arabia) the phrases "the empty money bag" and the "big oil company" were so tightly coupled together.
Surely, this must just be a coincidence!

Mark John Terranova

GE Locomotive being lifted by Crane

Gemini Ascending

The Broken Crane
(see Special Order on next page)

Mark John Terranova

BALDWIN - LIMA - HAMILTON CORPORATION
PHILADELPHIA, PA.

March 3, 1958

Mr. John M. Terranova
Master Mechanic
Saudi Government Railway
Dhahran, Saudi Arabia

Dear Mr. Terranova:

Reference is made to our letter of February 13, 1958 in which we notified you we had initiated our Inquiry No. 158-562 covering forty 30-cubic yard, 50-ton dual pivot air operated side dump drop door cars.

A quotation has now been prepared and presented to our Export Department for transmittal to Mr. J. H. Gildea.

If there are any developments on this particular order, we certainly would appreciate hearing from you and if there would be any information needed at your end, do not hesitate to drop the writer a line and he will see that same is forwarded to you immediately.

Very truly yours,

W. H. Dallas
Sales Department

WHD:dr

The Special Order for forty 50-ton air operated side dump rail cars used around the cities of Dammam, Abqaig and Ghawar.

The broken crane and this special order story always had many layers and nuances associated with it. More will be revealed in future books in this series.

Part of the Marching Band

Royal Railroad Dining Car with Bodyguards

The beautiful Date Palm Trees at Hofuf

Dad (John M. Terranova) on right
with character called Jahleel in Book 1.

CPSIA information can be obtained
at www.ICGtesting.com
Printed in the USA
LVOW13s0838011117
554572LV00003B/4/P